# SUN SOCIETY

## Laura Shenton

# SUN SOCIETY

## Laura Shenton

Iridescent Toad Publishing

Iridescent Toad Publishing.



Cover design by Artscandare.

First edition. ISBN 978-1-917969-05-5

# Chapter One

The cottage smelt of wilted herbs and desperation, which wasn't exactly the ambiance I'd been hoping for. I stood in the doorway of my father's room, my fingers gripping the worn wood of the frame hard enough that splinters threatened to bite into my palm. Inside, my mother Miriel fussed over him with the kind of determined energy that came from refusing to accept defeat. Her silver-streaked auburn hair had come loose from its braid, wisps clinging to her damp temples as she moved.

"Still no change?" I asked, though I already knew the answer from the way her shoulders sagged beneath her thin linen dress – the defeated curve of them making her look smaller than I'd ever seen her.

"He's breathing." Her voice was brittle. "That counts for something."

My throat tightened. My father, Jorik, lay propped against a collection of threadbare pillows. His normally olive complexion – the warm, sun-kissed tone I'd inherited – had faded to a concerning shade of pale green. His pointed ears, which had always been so expressive and mobile when he laughed or argued, now drooped against his dark hair. For an elf who'd spent his entire adult life insisting he was "too young to slow down", he looked decidedly slowed down. The wrongness of it made my stomach churn.

"The fever broke for about an hour yesterday," Mother said, wringing out a cloth in a basin of lukewarm water. Her knuckles were white with the effort. "I thought maybe..." She trailed off, apparently deciding that finishing hopeful sentences was too risky.

I stepped into the room, my bare feet silent on the worn wooden floor. "Mother," I said, settling onto the edge of the bed. "We need to talk about Healer Morvaine."

Mother's hands stilled on the cloth. The water dripped, each drop marking time like a countdown. "There's nothing to discuss. She's made her position clear."

Heat flashed through me, anger mixing with helplessness. "Her position is ridiculous. She's refusing to treat Father because you accidentally stepped on her prised roses. It was an innocent mistake, and we apologised."

"Apologising apparently wasn't enough." Mother's voice carried the bitter edge of someone who'd replayed the same conversation a dozen times, each replay carving the wound deeper. "She said our family has always been 'disrespectful of proper authority'."

I snorted, the sound sharp and unladylike. "Proper authority? She's a healer, not the village chief. Her job is to heal people, not hold grudges over garden mishaps."

"Her job is whatever she decides it is." Mother returned to her cloth-wringing with renewed vigour, her movements jerky with suppressed emotion. "She's the only healer in Miltoven. We need her more than she needs us."

This was the heart of our problem, and I'd been ruminating on it until my thoughts were raw. Miltoven was a small village where everyone knew everyone else's business, and everyone had accepted that magical healing was the exclusive domain of those who claimed to be "blessed" or "gifted". Healer Morvaine had been the only officially recognised healer for as long as anyone could remember, which meant she had the entire village over a barrel when it came to medical emergencies.

The fact that all elves technically had magical potential was apparently beside the point. According to village tradition, only those who were properly trained and officially designated could be trusted to use it. Everyone else was expected to stick to their assigned roles and not get ideas above their station.

"What if we went to the next village?" I suggested, though I already knew what Mother would say.

"They can't be relied upon," she said. "We don't know if their healer would even see us."

I looked at Father. He was sleeping fitfully, his breathing shallow and laboured, each exhale a rattling wheeze that made my own lungs ache in sympathy. He had always been the one to challenge unfair rules and question stupid traditions. If he were in good health, he'd probably be plotting to march over to Healer Morvaine's house and demand she do her job properly. But he wasn't well, and that left me to do the marching.

"Then I'll go further." The words came out suddenly, the decision crystallising in my mind as I spoke. "There must be other healers out there. Other villages, other options."

Mother dropped the cloth, its dampness darkening the floor. "Absolutely not."

"Why not?"

"Because you're my daughter, and I'm not losing both of you to this mess." Her voice carried a maternal authority that had kept me in line for most of my twenty-three years, but beneath it I heard the quaver of fear. "It's dangerous to travel alone, especially for a young elven woman."

"I'm not that young," I protested, even as part of me recognised how young I must seem to her – barely into adulthood by elven standards. "And I'm not helpless. I can take care of myself."

"Against bandits? Wild animals? Strange villages where no one knows you?" Her amber eyes – so like my own – were wide with panic.

I stood up, my legs suddenly restless, and paced to the small window that looked out over our vegetable garden. The late summer sun hung high in the afternoon sky, casting a warm, hazy light that should have been beautiful but instead felt melancholic. Our tomatoes were coming in nicely, their red globes heavy on the vine, but what was the point of a good harvest if Father wasn't going to be around to enjoy it? The thought made my eyes sting with unshed tears.

"Mother." I turned back to face her, and I let her see the fear and determination warring in my expression. "Father is dying."

The words hung in the air like a challenge, and saying them aloud made them more real, more terrifying. Mother's face crumpled slightly, the careful mask of hope she'd been wearing finally cracking.

"We can't keep hoping Healer Morvaine will change her mind," I pressed. "And we can't keep pretending that lukewarm cloths and herbal teas are going to cure whatever he has. He needs real help."

"And you think you can find it?" The question was barely a whisper.

"I think I have to try." I moved back to the bed, dropping to my knees beside her. The floor was hard and unforgiving beneath me, but I barely felt it. "Look at him, Mother. Really look at him. He's getting worse every day. If we do nothing, we're going to lose him."

Mother was quiet for a long moment, her eyes fixed on Father's face with an intensity that spoke of memorising, of preparing for loss. They had been married for over thirty years, and I'd grown up watching them navigate life with the kind of partnership that made other couples slightly envious. They argued about everything – politics, gardening techniques, the proper way to cook eggs – but they also supported each other through every crisis. The thought of my mother without my father, of that partnership severed, made my chest constrict with grief.

"If something happens to you out there," Mother said finally, her voice breaking, "I'll never forgive myself."

"And if I don't try, and Father dies, *I'll* never forgive myself." I reached for her hand, clasping it between both of mine. Her skin was cool and rough from work, familiar as my own heartbeat. "Mother, I have to do this. It's the right thing to do."

She closed her eyes, and I could practically see her weighing the risks against the alternatives, the terrible mathematics of love and loss. When she opened them again, tears clung to her lashes, but there was a resigned determination in her expression that made my own eyes burn in response.

"How long would you be gone?"

"I don't know. A few weeks, maybe? It depends on how far I have to travel to find help."

"And you'd go alone?"

"Unless you know someone who wants to join me on a quest to find healing for a family that most people think are too uppity for their own good?"

Despite everything, Mother smiled slightly at that, her expression tired but genuine. "You get your smart mouth from your father."

"I get my stubbornness from both of you." The words came out softer than I'd intended, affection warming them.

"If you're determined to do this, then we need to plan it properly. You'll need supplies, money, a good story about why you're travelling alone."

"You'll let me go?" I still hardly dared to believe it.

"I'll help you prepare to go," she corrected me. "There's a difference. I still think this is a terrible idea, but you're right about one thing: we can't just sit here and wait for a miracle."

We spent the next hour making lists and checking our modest savings, and with each item we discussed, the reality of what I was about to do settled more heavily around me.

I would take our best horse – Copper, with his gentle temperament and steady gait – along with enough essentials for several weeks of travel. Mother insisted on packing my travel bag with an assortment of items that ranged from practical (a sharp knife that had been my grandfather's, a warm cloak lined with rabbit fur) to sentimental (a small carved wooden bird that had been my favourite toy as a child, its wings worn smooth from countless hours of play).

"Promise me you'll be careful," Mother said. "Don't trust strangers too quickly, don't travel after dark, and if you run into trouble, come home immediately."

"I promise." I meant it with every fibre of my being. I had no intention of taking unnecessary risks, but neither was I willing to give up easily. The two imperatives would have to find balance somehow.

Father stirred briefly. His eyes opened and focused on me with unusual clarity.

"Elenah." His whisper was barely audible, his voice like dried leaves scraping across stone.

"I'm here, Father." I moved to his side, taking his hand. His skin was papery and hot, his fingers skeletal in my grip. The physical evidence of his decline made my throat close with emotion.

"Going somewhere?" he uttered weakly.

I glanced at Mother, who nodded encouragingly, her eyes glistening. "I'm going to find help," I said. "Real help."

Father's mouth curved into what might have been a smile, the ghost of his usual mischievous grin. "Good girl. Don't let anyone tell you what you can't do."

"I won't." I squeezed his hand gently, afraid of hurting him, afraid of never holding him again. "I'll come back as soon as I can."

"Take your time." He was already drifting back to sleep, his eyelids heavy. "Do it right."

# Chapter Two

The afternoon light slanted through the kitchen window as I worked my way through the pile of dishes that had accumulated over the past few days. My hands moved mechanically through the warm water, scrubbing at dried porridge that clung stubbornly to the bottom of a wooden bowl. In the next room, I could hear Mother's quiet murmurs as she tended to Father, her voice a constant, soothing presence that had become the soundtrack to our days.

I'd already swept the floors, beaten the rugs, and hauled fresh water from the well – anything to keep my hands busy and my mind from spiralling into the dozens of catastrophic possibilities that awaited me on the road. The physical labour helped, but only barely. Each task completed was one step closer to tomorrow, when I would actually have to leave.

The dishes clinked softly as I stacked them to dry. Outside, the sky was beginning to deepen from blue to purple, the first hints of dusk creeping across the horizon. My pulse quickened slightly, an involuntary response I'd developed over the past three years. Around this time, as darkness began to gather at the edges of the world, Nikola would finish his shift at the tavern and make his way to our cottage.

Like clockwork. Like coming home.

I dried my hands on my apron and moved to the front window, peering out at the path that led from the village centre. My heart did that ridiculous fluttering thing it always did when I thought about seeing him, even after all this time. Three years together, and he still made me feel shy and breathless, as if we'd only just met.

I was just about to turn away when I saw him – tall and lean, moving with an easy grace that made him unmistakable even in the fading light. Nikola's dark hair caught the last rays of sun, and he carried something carefully in his hands, his focus on not spilling whatever it was. Even from this distance, even in silhouette, he was beautiful in a way that made my chest ache. Strong, capable features that somehow managed to be both rugged and refined. The kind of face that made strangers look twice and then keep looking.

But it was more than his appearance. It was the way he moved through the world – confident but not arrogant, aware of his own appeal but not consumed by it. Intelligent eyes that noticed everything, hands that were equally comfortable wielding a lute as they were hauling barrels or mending a broken chair. And his voice – gods, his voice. Rich and warm, it could fill a room or wrap around you like a blanket, depending on what the moment required.

I was already at the door before he knocked, pulling it open with perhaps too much eagerness. The smile that lit his face made my breath catch, soft and familiar as a touch I'd been waiting for all day.

"Elenah." My name on his lips always sounded like something precious. His eyes – that remarkable shade of green-gold – searched my face with immediate concern.

He always could read me too well. "I brought something."

He lifted the covered pot he'd been carrying, and the rich, savoury smell of chicken soup wafted towards me. My stomach growled embarrassingly, reminding me that I'd been too anxious to eat much today.

"Nikola, you didn't have to..."

"I know I didn't have to." He stepped inside, and I caught the familiar scent of him – woodsmoke and soap and something that was just uniquely his. "But Marta made extra at the tavern for tonight, and when I told her it was for your father, she packed enough to feed half the village."

Mother appeared in the doorway of Father's room, and her tired face brightened when she saw what Nikola carried. "Is that Marta's chicken soup?"

"Still hot from the kitchen," Nikola confirmed, moving to set it on our small table. "She added extra herbs. Said they're good for strength."

"Bless that woman." Mother came forward, clasping Nikola's hand in both of hers. "And bless you for thinking of us. This is exactly what Jorik needs."

The gratitude in her voice made my throat tight. We'd become the kind of family that survived on the kindness of others, and whilst I was grateful, part of me hated the necessity of it. Hated that we'd been reduced to this because one petty healer couldn't let go of crushed roses.

"It's nothing," Nikola said, though we all knew it wasn't. Working at the tavern, he probably got one decent meal a day as part of his wages, and he still thought to bring food to us. "How is he today?"

"The same." Mother's voice was carefully neutral. "Which is to say, not good, but not worse."

I watched Nikola's jaw tighten, saw the flash of anger and helplessness cross his features before he smoothed them away. He knew as well as I did what Father's condition meant, what it said about the injustice of our situation.

"Nikola," I said, my voice coming out quieter than I'd intended. "Can we go for a walk? I need to talk to you about something."

His eyes found mine, and I saw understanding dawn there – nothing good ever followed that particular phrasing. But he nodded, his expression gentle. "Of course."

Mother looked between us, her face softening with sympathy. She knew what I had to tell him. "Don't be gone too long. It's already getting late."

"We won't," I promised.

I grabbed my shawl from its hook by the door, and Nikola held it for me as I wrapped it around my shoulders – a small, courteous gesture that he'd done a thousand times and still made me feel cared for. His fingers brushed the back of my neck as he helped settle the fabric, and I shivered despite the warmth of the evening.

We walked in silence down the familiar path that led away from the cottage, towards the old oak tree where someone had built a wooden swing bench years before I was born.

The chains creaked slightly in the evening breeze, and the seat had been worn smooth by countless hours of use. Nikola and I had claimed it as ours three years ago. We'd spent more evenings there than I could count – talking, laughing, sharing dreams and fears under the stars.

I settled onto the bench, and Nikola sat beside me, close enough that our thighs pressed together. He set the swing in motion with one foot, the gentle rocking immediately familiar and soothing. For a long moment, neither of us spoke. I watched the last light drain from the sky, painting everything in shades of indigo and violet.

"You're leaving," Nikola said finally, his voice quiet but certain.

I turned to look at him, surprised. "How did you..."

"I know you, Elenah." His smile was sad, perceptive. "I saw the determined look on your face when I arrived. And I know you've been trying to work out how to save your father." He reached for my hand, lacing our fingers together. "You're going to find a healer."

"I have to." The words came out thick with emotion. "Mother agreed. I'm leaving tomorrow morning, taking Copper, enough supplies for a few weeks. I'll go as far as I need to until I find someone who can help."

Nikola was quiet, his thumb tracing circles on the back of my hand. I watched him, taking in the strong line of his nose, the curve of his lips, the set of his jaw – all of it taut with the effort of holding himself together.

"I want to come with you," he said finally, and the rawness in his voice nearly broke me. "Gods, Elenah, you have to know I want to come with you."

"I know." I squeezed his hand. "But your parents..."

"Need me here." He finished the thought, his voice bitter with frustration. "My father's back isn't getting any better, and my mother can barely manage the house on her own now. The wages from the tavern are all that's keeping them fed and housed."

I knew this. We both knew this. Nikola was twenty-six and should have been out building his own life, pursuing his own dreams, but instead he was trapped by duty and love and the simple, crushing economics of survival. His parents had no one else. He couldn't abandon them.

"It's not fair," I whispered, though I hated how childish the words sounded.

"No, it's not." Nikola turned to face me more fully, his free hand coming up to cup my cheek. His palm was warm and rough from work, achingly familiar. "But you have to help your father, and I have to take care of mine. That's just how it is."

"I wish…" My voice broke, and I had to stop, swallow, try again. "I wish we could just be together. No complications, no impossible choices."

"We are together." His thumb brushed across my cheekbone, catching a tear that had escaped despite my best efforts. "Distance doesn't change that. A few weeks apart doesn't change that."

"A few weeks." I tried to make my voice sound confident, certain, but it came out small and frightened instead. "That's all it'll be. I'll find someone, bring them back, and everything will go back to normal."

We both knew I was lying. Nothing about this was certain, and normal felt like something from another lifetime. But Nikola didn't challenge me. Instead, he pulled me closer, wrapping his arm around my shoulders so my head rested against his chest. I could hear his heartbeat, steady and strong, and I tried to memorise the sound of it.

"You're going to be fine," he said, his voice rumbling through his chest. "You're the strongest person I know, Elenah. Smart, capable, stubborn as a mule when you need to be."

Despite everything, I laughed against his shirt. "That's romantic."

"It's true." His lips pressed against the top of my head. "You're going to go out there, find exactly what you need, and come home to us. To me."

I wanted to believe him. Needed to believe him. But the fear was there, cold and insistent, reminding me of all the things that could go wrong. "What if I can't? What if I fail?"

"You won't." His certainty should have felt false, but somehow it didn't. "But if things get too dangerous, if you can't find help, then you come home. Your father wouldn't want you risking your life."

I pulled back enough to look up at him, beautiful and beloved and about to be out of reach. "I'm going to miss you. So much."

"I'm going to miss you too." His voice was rough with emotion. "Every day. Every shift at the tavern, every evening, every night. I'll be counting the hours until you come back."

The ache in my chest was physical, painful. I wanted to tell him I loved him, but the words could not convey the enormity of what I felt. Three years together since I was twenty, and he'd become as essential to me as breathing. The thought of being apart from him, of not seeing his face or hearing his voice, felt impossible.

"Sing to me?" The request came out small, almost childish, but I needed it. Needed the comfort that only his voice could provide. "Please?"

Nikola's expression softened, and he adjusted his hold on me, settling me more comfortably against his side. "Any requests?"

"Something hopeful," I whispered. "Something about coming home."

He was quiet for a moment, thinking, and then he began to sing. His voice was low and rich, the notes pure and clear. It was a song I'd heard before, an old elven ballad about a wanderer who travelled far from home but always found their way back to the one they loved. The melody was sweet and slightly melancholy, and his voice wrapped around me like a warm embrace.

I closed my eyes, letting the sound wash over me. This was what I would miss most, I thought. Not just Nikola's presence, but moments like this – the two of us suspended in our own small world, his voice and my heartbeat the only things that mattered. He sang the whole song through, and when the last note faded into the darkness, neither of us moved. We just sat there, holding each other, the swing creaking gently beneath us.

"I love you," I said finally, because the words needed to be said even if they couldn't capture everything. "Whatever happens, I need you to know that."

"I know." His arms tightened around me. "And I love you. Always have, always will. That's not going to change just because you're gone for a little while."

He pulled back enough to tilt my chin up, and then his lips were on mine – soft and beautifully familiar. The kiss was gentle, sweet, tinged with desperation and longing. When we finally pulled apart, both of us were breathing harder, and I had to resist the urge to pull him back, to lose myself in him and forget about everything else.

But I couldn't forget. Tomorrow was coming, whether I was ready or not.

"I should get back," I said reluctantly. "Mother will worry."

"I know," he said. But we didn't move immediately. We sat there a moment longer, neither wanting to be the first to break the spell.

Finally, Nikola stood and pulled me to my feet. We walked back to the cottage hand in hand, and I tried to memorise the feel of his fingers laced with mine, the way his stride matched perfectly with my own, the comfortable silence that had always existed between us.

At the door, he pulled me into one last embrace, his face buried in my hair. "Be careful," he murmured. "Come back to me."

"I will." I clung to him, breathing in his scent one more time. "I promise."

He kissed me once more – harder this time, more urgent – and then he was pulling away, stepping back into the darkness. I watched him go, his form disappearing down the path, and I stood there long after he'd vanished from sight, my hand pressed against my lips where I could still feel the ghost of his kiss.

When I finally went inside, Mother took one look at my face and pulled me into a hug. She didn't say anything, just held me whilst I cried quietly against her shoulder, mourning the goodbye I'd just lived through and dreading the ones still to come.

***

That night as I lay in bed, my eyes fixed on the wooden beams above, sleep felt impossible. My mind raced with possibilities and concerns, each thought branching into a dozen more until my head spun with the momentum of unknowns.

Tomorrow, I would leave everything familiar behind and venture into the wider world in search of healing for my father. The thought was terrifying and empowering in equal measure, a dizzying combination that left me feeling unmoored. I'd never been more than a day's travel from Miltoven, never had to navigate foreign customs or negotiate with strangers who might not have my best interests at heart. What if I got lost? What if I ran out of money? What if the other villages were just as unhelpful as Healer Morvaine?

I thought about Nikola, the way his voice had wrapped around me like protection. I thought about Father lying in the next room, his breathing laboured even in sleep. I thought about Mother's tired eyes and the worry on her shoulders.

I rolled onto my side, clutching my pillow, and tried to calm my racing thoughts. Sleep would come eventually. It had to. Tomorrow would be difficult enough without facing it exhausted.

As I finally began to drift off, my mind slowing and softening at the edges, my last conscious thought was a prayer to whatever forces governed the universe: *Let me find what I'm looking for. And let me find it in time.*

The darkness rose up to meet me, and I surrendered to it, hoping that when I woke, I would find the courage I would need to face everything that lay ahead.

# Chapter Three

I left at dawn, when mist still hung low over the fields and the village was barely stirring. The world was painted in shades of grey and silver, everything soft-edged and dreamlike. I'd said my goodbyes quickly, not trusting myself to maintain my resolve. Even now, as Copper and I made our way down the familiar path, I could feel the pull of home behind me – a physical tug at my chest that urged me to turn around, to go back where it was safe and known.

But I kept my eyes forward and my jaw set. Father needed help. That was all that mattered.

Copper, sturdy and intuitive, seemed to sense the importance of our mission. He stepped out briskly onto the dirt road that led away from Miltoven, his ears pricked forward with interest rather than reluctance. His copper-coloured coat gleamed even in the dim light, and I felt a rush of gratitude for his steady presence. At least I wasn't completely alone.

"Well, boy," I said, patting his warm neck as we crested the hill that marked the edge of our familiar territory, "it's just you and me now. Try not to let it go to your head."

Copper snorted, his breath visible in the cool morning air, and I chose to interpret it as agreement rather than scepticism. Behind us, Miltoven disappeared into the mist, and with it, everything I'd ever known. The finality of it sent a shiver down my spine that had nothing to do with the morning chill.

The first day of travel was uneventful, which was exactly what I'd been hoping for. I followed the main road south, reasoning that larger roads led to larger towns, and larger towns were more likely to have multiple healers. The weather was pleasant, and the scenery was pretty enough to keep me entertained. Rolling fields gave way to small copses of trees, and occasionally I'd pass a farmhouse or catch sight of workers in distant fields. Copper maintained a steady pace that ate up the miles without wearing either of us out, his hoofbeats a rhythmic accompaniment to my churning thoughts.

I stopped for lunch beside a small stream, the water clear and cold over smooth stones. I shared my bread and cheese with Copper, who took his portion with gentle lips, whilst I studied the map Mother had given me. The parchment was old and worn at the creases, but the roads and towns were clearly marked. Two towns I'd never heard of were marked along my route: Fernbridge, two days south, and Oakenford, a day beyond that. If neither could help, I'd have to ask locals for directions to others. The thought of venturing even further from home made my stomach clench with anxiety, but I pushed it aside. Whatever it took. However far I needed to go.

"The trick," I told Copper as we resumed our journey, his reins loose in my hands, "is not to look too desperate. Desperate people get taken advantage of. We want to look like we have options."

Copper flicked an ear back at me, and I smiled despite myself. Talking to my horse was probably a sign that I was already going a little mad from solitude, but it was better than the silence.

The next day was cloudier and cooler, with a persistent breeze that made me grateful for my warm cloak. I pulled it tighter around my shoulders, the fur lining soft against my neck. I encountered more traffic on the road – merchants leading pack animals laden with goods, farmers heading to market with carts full of produce, a family of elves travelling in a well-maintained wagon, nodding politely as they passed without stopping to chat. Each time I passed someone, my heart would speed up slightly, hyperaware of being a young woman travelling alone. But no one bothered me, and gradually I began to relax, to feel less like prey and more like just another traveller on the road.

It was mid-afternoon the following day when I finally saw the smoke rising from Fernbridge's chimneys. My heart lifted with anticipation, hope fluttering in my chest. This was my first real test: could I find what I needed in a town where no one knew me or cared about my family's problems? Where I was just another stranger passing through?

Fernbridge turned out to be a bustling place, at least by Miltoven standards. The buildings were larger, more prosperous-looking than those back home. There were shops selling everything from leather goods to imported spices, their colourful signs swinging in the breeze. The air smelt of baking bread and horse manure and something sweet I couldn't quite identify. People moved with purpose, calling greetings to each other, haggling over prices, living their lives in a way that made Miltoven seem sleepy and small by comparison.

I found a stable for Copper and enquired about lodging for the night, trying to project confidence whilst fighting off the nervous flutter in my stomach. My hands wanted to twist in Copper's mane, to fidget with my cloak, to betray how out of my depth I felt. Instead, I kept them still and my voice steady.

"You'll want The Silver Acorn," the stable master told me, jerking his thumb towards a two-storey building with painted green shutters. The elven man's hair was streaked with premature grey from years of outdoor work, and his hands were gnarled but gentle as he took Copper's reins. "Clean beds, decent food, and they don't ask too many questions about single women travelling alone."

I felt my cheeks warm slightly at the implication, but I was grateful for the discretion. "Perfect. And if I were looking for a healer?"

The stable master's expression grew thoughtful, his weathered face creasing with concern. "Well, there's Healer Aldric, but he's been a bit... temperamental lately. His wife left him last month, and he's been drowning his sorrows in ale ever since. It might not be the best time to need his services."

My heart sank like a stone. Of course. Of course even here, away from Miltoven, the healers would be unreliable. "Is there anyone else?"

"There's a wise woman named Grandmother Holda who lives on the outskirts of town. She's not officially a healer, but she knows her herbs and potions. Some folks swear by her remedies."

"Officially a healer?" I repeated, recognising the familiar refrain. The same barriers, the same arbitrary rules, even here.

"Well, you know how it is." The stable master shrugged, leading Copper towards an empty stall. "The Healers' Guild doesn't recognise anyone who hasn't been through their formal training. But between you and me, Grandmother Holda has probably saved more lives than half the Guild-certified healers I've met."

This was interesting. I'd heard references to the Healers' Guild before. Apparently, a small group of people had declared themselves the only legitimate practitioners of healing magic, and everyone else was expected to defer to their authority.

"Where would I find Grandmother Holda?" I asked, watching as he settled Copper with fresh hay and water.

"Take the east road out of town for about a mile. Keep your eyes peeled for a cottage with a garden that looks like it's trying to take over the world. You can't miss it."

I thanked him, pressing a few coins into his palm, and headed for The Silver Acorn, my spirits considerably improved. Maybe this journey wouldn't be as difficult as I'd feared. Maybe there were people out here who didn't bow to arbitrary authority.

The Silver Acorn lived up to its reputation: clean, comfortable, and staffed by people who seemed genuinely pleased to have guests. The common room was warm and inviting, with a fire crackling in the hearth and the smell of roasted meat making my mouth water. I secured a room for the night – a small but tidy space with a real bed and clean linens – and came back down to enjoy my first hot meal in days.

The food was simple but delicious: roasted chicken with root vegetables, fresh bread still warm from the oven, and a mug of cider that was sweet and slightly tart. I ate slowly, savouring every bite, listening to the conversations flowing around me. Most of the talk was standard tavern fare – complaints about the weather, gossip about local politics, speculation about whether the harvest would be good this year.

Somewhere in the corner, a musician was playing a lively tune on a fiddle, and several patrons had started clapping along. The music was cheerful and infectious, and I found myself tapping my foot beneath the table. If Nikola were here with me, I thought with a pang of longing, he would probably be singing along quietly and romantically in my ear, his warm breath tickling my neck, making me laugh despite the seriousness of our mission. The thought made me miss him.

A thread of conversation from a nearby table drew my attention, cutting through my melancholy. "I'm telling you, Daysi," one of the women said, "my cousin's baby would have died if she'd waited for Guild Healer Aldric to sober up enough to see her. Grandmother Holda had that fever broken in two hours."

"That's all well and good," Daysi replied, scepticism clear in her tone, "but what happens when someone gets seriously hurt and needs real healing? Herbal teas and poultices can only do so much."

"Who says Grandmother Holda only uses herbal teas?"

I finished my meal quickly, wiping my mouth with the cloth napkin, and approached the two women, trying to look casual rather than desperate for information. My heart hammered in my chest, but I kept my expression friendly and open.

"Excuse me," I said, stopping beside their table. "I couldn't help overhearing your conversation. I'm looking for healing help for my father, and someone mentioned Grandmother Holda. Would you mind telling me more about her?"

The first woman, a middle-aged elf with laughter lines around her eyes and silver threading through her auburn hair, smiled warmly. The expression immediately put me at ease. "Oh, she's wonderful. She's been helping folks in this area for longer than anyone can remember. What's wrong with your father?"

I described Father's symptoms as best I could, trying not to dwell on how much worse he'd looked when I left – the pallor of his skin, the laboured breathing, the way his eyes had barely focused on me when we said goodbye. Both women listened with the kind of attention that made me feel heard rather than dismissed, their faces showing genuine concern rather than judgement or dismissal.

"That does sound serious," Daysi admitted, her earlier scepticism giving way to sympathy.

"Is Grandmother Holda... officially trained?" I asked carefully, not wanting to offend but needing to know what I was dealing with.

The two women exchanged a look that spoke volumes – a mix of amusement and something more guarded, more knowing.

"Let's just say she doesn't advertise her qualifications," the first woman said diplomatically, leaning in slightly as if sharing a secret. "But her results speak for themselves. If your father needs help, she's your best chance in this town."

Relief washed over me, so intense it made my knees weak. I thanked them profusely – probably more than the situation warranted – and retired to my room, feeling cautiously optimistic.

The small room felt both confining and liberating – a space that was mine but not mine, temporary and transient. I undressed slowly, hanging my travel-stained clothes over the chair, and slipped into the narrow bed. The mattress was softer than mine at home, the sheets smelling faintly of lavender.

I fell asleep thinking about Father, hoping he was still fighting, still breathing, still waiting for me to return with the help he needed.

# Chapter Four

Grandmother Holda's cottage was exactly as advertised: a modest stone building almost entirely overwhelmed by what appeared to be a botanical explosion. Vines covered the walls in thick curtains of green, their leaves rustling softly in the breeze. Herb gardens sprawled in every direction – neat rows giving way to wild tangles of plants that seemed to grow wherever they pleased. Fruit trees heavy with late-season apples created a dappled canopy over the entire property, their branches so laden they nearly touched the ground. It looked like the kind of place where nature had been invited to make itself completely at home, and had accepted the invitation with enthusiasm.

I tied Copper to a fence post and picked my way through the garden, trying not to step on anything that looked particularly valuable.

My boots crunched on the gravel path, which was barely visible beneath creeping thyme and mint. The air was thick with scent – sharp and sweet and green all at once – a dozen different plants I couldn't identify mingling together in a perfume that made my head swim slightly. Everything here felt alive, humming with growth and potential.

Before I could knock, the door swung open to reveal a small, ancient-looking elf with silver hair braided down her back and the most mischievous eyes I'd ever seen. They were dark and bright simultaneously, like polished river stones, and they seemed to take in everything about me in a single glance. Her face was a map of wrinkles, each line telling a story, and her smile revealed teeth that were remarkably straight for someone of her evident age.

"You must be the girl looking for help with her father," Grandmother Holda said without preamble, her voice surprisingly strong and clear. "I heard you were in town asking questions."

I blinked, taken aback by her directness. "Word travels fast."

"Small town, big ears," Grandmother Holda replied cheerfully, stepping aside to let me pass. "Come in, come in. Tell me about this father of yours whilst I make tea."

The inside of the cottage was as cluttered and comfortable as the outside was overgrown. Every surface was covered with jars, bottles, dried herbs hanging in bunches from the ceiling beams, and mysterious objects that might have been magical or might have been decorative – or possibly both. The walls were lined with shelves that sagged under the weight of books and curiosities. A fire crackled in the hearth. The warmth of the space wrapped around me like an embrace. This place felt safe.

Grandmother Holda bustled around her kitchen with surprising speed for someone who looked ancient enough to have witnessed the planting of those apple trees outside. She assembled tea and pastries whilst I described Father's condition in detail – the fever that came and went, the terrible pallor, the way his breathing had become increasingly laboured, the horrible greenish tinge to his skin.

"Hmm..." the old woman mused. "It sounds like lung fever with complications. Nasty business, but treatable if you know what you're doing." She fixed me with a sharp look that made me feel suddenly transparent, as if she could see right through to my bones. "Your village healer wouldn't see him?"

"She's... holding a grudge." The admission tasted bitter on my tongue. I explained about the roses, about Healer Morvaine's vindictiveness, and with each word I felt my anger rekindling.

Grandmother Holda made a disgusted noise, her expression hardening. "Healers who let personal feelings interfere with their work should find a different purpose entirely. Preferably something that doesn't involve other people's lives." She poured tea into mismatched cups – one painted with flowers, the other plain ceramic – and settled into the chair across from me with a satisfied sigh. "So what makes you think I can help?"

"Honestly? Desperation." I decided candour was probably my best strategy with this woman who seemed to see through pretence like glass. "But also, people in town say you get results."

"I do get results," Grandmother Holda agreed without false modesty, taking a sip of her tea. "But not because I'm more talented than other healers. I get results because I'm not hung up on stupid rules about who's allowed to heal and how they're allowed to do it."

This was promising. "What do you mean?"

Grandmother Holda sipped her tea thoughtfully, her eyes studying me over the rim of her cup. "How much do you know about the way healing magic actually works?"

"Not much," I admitted, feeling suddenly ignorant. "In our village, we're taught that only specially trained healers can use magic safely, and that everyone else should leave it to the experts."

"Rubbish." Grandmother Holda said the word flatly, with such finality that I almost laughed. "All elves have magical ability. The only difference is that healers are taught a specific set of techniques and told they're the only ones that work." She set down her cup with a decisive clink.

"Are they the only ones that work?" I leant forward, my pastry forgotten on my plate.

"Goodness, no." Grandmother Holda stood up with surprising grace and moved to one of her many shelves, her fingers trailing along the jars until she found what she was looking for. She pulled down a container filled with what looked like thin, brittle curls of bark. "This is willow bark. Excellent for reducing fever and inflammation. I could prepare it as a simple tea, which any village grandmother might do, or I could enhance it with magic to make it more effective." She held up the jar, the contents rustling softly. "The magic doesn't care whether I learnt it at a formal academy or worked it out myself through trial and error. Magic responds to intent and will, not credentials."

I felt a spark of something that might have been hope – fragile and bright. "So you could help my father?"

"I could try." Grandmother Holda's expression grew more serious, and my hope flickered. "But here's the thing: I can't just hand you a potion and send you on your way. Lung fever is serious business, and treating it properly requires more than one dose of medicine. Your father would need ongoing care, probably for several weeks. Daily monitoring, adjustments to the treatment, constant vigilance."

My heart sank. "I can't bring him here. He's too sick to travel. The journey alone would probably kill him."

"And I can't go to your village." Grandmother Holda's voice was genuinely apologetic, her eyes sympathetic. "I'm too old for long journeys – my bones wouldn't survive the distance – and besides, your official healer probably wouldn't appreciate the competition. These territorial types tend to get nasty when their authority is challenged."

We sat in silence for a moment, both considering the problem. The fire popped and hissed. I felt frustration building in my throat, threatening to spill over into tears. I'd come so far, been so hopeful, and now...

"There might be another option," Grandmother Holda said slowly, interrupting my spiral into despair.

"Oh?"

"Have you ever heard of the Sun Society?"

"No. What is it?" The name meant nothing to me, but the way she said it – with a mixture of respect and intrigue – made my pulse quicken.

Her eyes lit up with genuine enthusiasm, the mischievous sparkle returning. "A group of elves who live in Thornwood Forest, about three days' travel east of here. They've completely rejected the idea that healing should be limited to official practitioners. Everyone in their community learns basic medical skills, and they've developed some remarkable techniques. Collaborative magic."

"Collaborative magic?" I'd never heard the term before. The magic I knew about was solitary, individual – one healer working on one patient.

"Instead of relying on one healer to do everything, they work together, pooling their magical energy to achieve better results. It's quite revolutionary, actually." Grandmother Holda leant forward conspiratorially, lowering her voice as if sharing a dangerous secret. "The Healers' Guild can't stand them, but I've seen some of their work. I knew a woman whose child was dying – a wasting sickness that three Guild healers had declared incurable. The Sun Society saved that child's life. Impressive doesn't begin to cover it."

Hope surged back stronger than before. "And you think they might help?"

"I think they might do more than help." Grandmother Holda's smile was knowing, almost cunning. "I think they might teach you how to help your father yourself."

The idea was both thrilling and terrifying. "Me? But I don't know anything about healing magic. I've never even tried to use magic itself."

"You know more than you think." Grandmother Holda's voice was gentle now, almost tender. "Magic isn't some mysterious force that only works for special people. It's a natural ability that every elf possesses. It's in your blood, in your bones, as natural as breathing. The hard part isn't learning how to use it – the hard part is unlearning all the nonsense you've been taught about why you can't use it."

I stared into my tea, studying the leaves at the bottom of the cup. Everything I'd been told to believe about magic and healing was apparently wrong. The rigid structure of my world was cracking, revealing possibilities I'd never imagined. The question was whether I had the courage to act on this knowledge – to reach for something I'd been told my entire life was beyond me.

"How would I find these Sun Society people?" I asked.

"Ah, well, that's where things get a bit tricky," Grandmother Holda admitted, her expression turning more serious. "They don't exactly advertise their location. The Healers' Guild considers them a threat, and some of the more traditional communities have been known to give them trouble."

"What kind of trouble?"

"The kind where angry mobs show up with torches and strong opinions about how magic should be used." Grandmother Holda's tone was dry, but her eyes were hard. "Nothing that would deter truly determined people, but enough to make them cautious about strangers. They have to be careful about who they let in, who they trust. Can't blame them, really."

This was getting complicated. My initial hope was being tempered by practical concerns. "So how am I supposed to find them?"

Grandmother Holda smiled mysteriously, that mischievous glint returning to her eyes. "You could start by going to The Wanderer's Rest. It's a tavern, about a day's travel east towards the forest. It's a popular stopping point for travellers, and sometimes you meet interesting people there. People who might know about alternative approaches to healing. People who might recognise a genuine seeker when they see one."

"That's not very specific."

"The best opportunities rarely are," Grandmother Holda said philosophically, reaching over to pat my hand with her gnarled fingers. Her skin was paper-thin and warm, her touch surprisingly comforting. "But I have a good feeling about you, dear. You've got the right attitude for this sort of thing."

"Oh?" I uttered, genuinely curious.

"Stubborn determination mixed with a healthy disrespect for stupid rules." Grandmother

Holda grinned, the expression making her look decades younger. "It's exactly what you need for dealing with the Sun Society. They don't suffer fools, but they respect people who think for themselves."

I finished the last of my tea, the liquid getting cooler as we talked. My world felt bigger now, full of possibilities I hadn't known existed last night. The sun was already starting to slant through the cottage windows at a sharper angle, reminding me that time was passing – that with every hour, Father might be getting worse. I stood, knowing I needed to get moving, urgency thrumming through my veins.

"Thank you," I said, and I meant it with my whole heart. "For the information, and for... well, for making me think differently about things. For giving me hope."

"That's what old women are for," Grandmother Holda said with a wink, rising to see me out. "Shaking up young people's assumptions. Now go. Time waits for no elf, and your father needs you." She clasped my hands briefly, her grip surprisingly strong. "I'll be thinking of you and yours. May the road rise to meet you, child."

# Chapter Five

The Wanderer's Rest looked exactly like what I'd imagined: slightly shabby around the edges, welcoming in a rough-and-tumble way, and filled with the kind of comfortable noise that suggested everyone was having a good time whether they'd planned to or not. The wooden sign creaked on rusty hinges, and the windows glowed with warm lamplight that spilt out onto the dusty road.

I arrived in the late afternoon after a day of travel that had taken me progressively deeper into unfamiliar territory. The landscape had grown wilder and more forested, the cultivated fields giving way to dense stands of oak and elm. I'd passed fewer travellers on the road – just a lone merchant with his cart that morning, and a pair of elven hunters in the afternoon who'd nodded but not spoken. Copper seemed to enjoy the change of scenery, his ears pricked forward with interest at every new sound and smell. But I felt increasingly aware of how far I'd come from everything familiar, a knot of anxiety tightening in my stomach with each mile.

The tavern's main room was crowded with the usual mix of merchants, farmers, and travellers, their voices creating a pleasant hum of conversation. The air was thick with the smell of roasted meat, woodsmoke, and ale. But there was something different about the atmosphere here – something I couldn't quite name. People seemed more relaxed, more willing to strike up conversations with strangers. Laughter came easily, and no one seemed to be watching their neighbours with the suspicious wariness I was used to in Miltoven. Maybe it was the remoteness of the location, or maybe it was just the kind of place that attracted open-minded people.

I secured a room for the night – another small but clean space – and ordered dinner, trying to decide how to approach the delicate task of asking questions about secretive forest communities without sounding like either a spy or a lunatic. My mind spun with possible conversation starters, each one sounding more awkward than the last.

As it turned out, I didn't have to worry about making conversation. Conversation found me.

"Mind if I sit?" asked a cheerful voice, prompting me to look up from my plate.

A young elven woman about my own age stood there, and I felt my breath catch slightly in my throat. She had wildly curly auburn hair that seemed determined to escape from a colourful woven headband, several shades ranging from copper to deep red catching the lamplight. Her clothes were practical but eclectic – a worn leather vest over a shirt that might once have been white, trousers that had clearly seen hard use, and scuffed boots that looked like they'd walked a thousand miles.

But it was her face that held my attention: high cheekbones, a scattering of freckles across her nose, eyes that sparkled with intelligence and mischief in equal measure. She had the kind of beauty that came from living fully rather than carefully – the scruffy, unselfconscious attractiveness of someone who was too busy being useful to worry about appearances. A small silver hoop glinted in one pointed ear, and there was a thin scar running through her left eyebrow that only made her more striking.

"Please do," I said, trying to ignore the unexpected flutter in my chest. I was being ridiculous. I had Nikola. I was here for Father. This stranger's magnetic energy was just… surprising, that's all.

The newcomer slid into the opposite chair with the easy confidence of someone who was comfortable anywhere, sprawling slightly in her seat like a cat claiming territory. "I'm Traola," she said, extending her hand with that bright, encouraging smile that somehow made the whole room feel warmer.

"Elenah." I shook her hand. Her grip was firm and warm, her skin rough with calluses – the kind earned through tools, labour, and practical work.

"Travelling alone?" Traola asked, though her tone was curious rather than judgemental. She leant forward, genuinely interested. "That's either very brave or very foolish."

"Probably a bit of both," I admitted, and found myself relaxing despite the strange pull I felt towards this woman. There was something immediately trustworthy about her, something that invited honesty. "I'm looking for someone who can help my father. He's sick, and our village healer won't treat him."

Traola's expression shifted from casual interest to genuine concern, her smile fading into something more serious. "That's terrible. What kind of healer refuses to treat someone who's sick?"

"The kind who holds grudges over minor garden accidents." And suddenly I was telling the whole story to this sympathetic stranger – about Father's illness, about Healer Morvaine's pettiness, about my journey so far. There was something about Traola that invited confidences. She listened with complete attention, her expressive face showing every emotion the story evoked, making encouraging noises at all the right moments. When she was focused on me like this, I felt simultaneously visible and safe, seen without being judged.

"So you've been travelling around looking for alternative healers," she summarised when I finished, her voice warm with sympathy. "That's quite an undertaking."

"It's starting to feel like a bigger undertaking than I bargained for," I said. "I met this wonderful woman, Grandmother Holda, who told me about something called the Sun Society. Have you ever heard of them?"

Traola's eyes lit up with unmistakable recognition and delight, her whole face transforming. "The Sun Society? Oh, you're in luck. I know them quite well."

My heart skipped a beat, hope surging through me with almost painful intensity. "Really? Grandmother Holda said they might be able to help, but she wasn't sure of their exact location, and I'm worried I might not be able to find them."

"Finding them is the easy part," Traola said with a grin that made her look even more attractive. I felt my cheeks warm slightly and took a drink of my water to cover it. "The hard part is usually convincing them that you're not going to cause trouble. They've had some bad experiences with visitors who don't approve of their methods."

"What kind of methods?" I leant in closer, drawn by her enthusiasm as much as by the information.

Traola mirrored my posture, leaning forward conspiratorially, and I caught a scent of something herbal clinging to her clothes. "The Sun Society doesn't believe in the artificial scarcity that most communities impose on healing. Everyone learns basic medical skills, they share knowledge freely, and they use collaborative magic techniques that the Healers' Guild pretends are impossible."

This sounded exactly like what Grandmother Holda had described, and exactly like what I'd been hoping to find. "And you think they might help my father?"

"I think they might do better than that." Traola's eyes sparkled with conviction. "They might teach you how to help your father yourself. That's their whole philosophy: instead of making people dependent on a few designated healers, they believe everyone should have the knowledge and skills to take care of their community."

"That sounds almost too good to be true." I wanted to believe it, but previous disappointment had taught me caution.

"It's not too good to be true, it's just too good for some people's comfort," Traola said, passion creeping into her voice. "Which is why they keep a low profile. But if you're genuinely looking for help rather than wanting to cause problems, I think they'd be happy to meet you."

I felt a surge of hope mixed with nervous excitement, my hands trembling slightly where they rested on my lap. "Would you... would you be willing to introduce me to them?"

"Actually," Traola said, her smile widening into something brilliant, "I was planning to head back there tomorrow anyway. I'd be happy to have travelling company."

"Back there?" I repeated, my mind suddenly racing. Then the pieces clicked together. "You're part of the Sun Society?"

"Guilty as charged." Traola said it cheerfully, spreading her hands in an open gesture. "I was visiting some friends in the area and decided to stop here for the night. Good thing I did – this sounds like exactly the kind of situation we exist to help with."

I stared at Traola, hardly believing my luck. After days of uncertain searching, the solution to my problem had literally walked up and introduced itself. And she was charismatic and knowledgeable and far too distracting for my peace of mind.

"This is incredible," I said, my voice coming out slightly breathless. "I mean, what are the chances?"

"Better than you might think." Traola flagged down the server with an easy wave. "We tend to attract people who are questioning the way things are supposed to work. And you've got that look."

"What look?"

"The look of someone who's ready to discover that most of the rules they've been following are optional." She ordered drinks for both of us, then turned back to me, her full attention once again focused on me in that intense way that made my pulse quicken. "So tell me more about your father's condition. The more I know, the better I can explain the situation when we get to the settlement."

We spent the next hour discussing medical details, and I was impressed by how knowledgeable Traola was about healing. She asked intelligent questions, made useful suggestions about what the symptoms might indicate, and displayed the kind of practical competence that came from real experience rather than just theory. As she talked, she gestured expressively with her hands, and I found myself watching the play of lamplight across her animated features.

"You really know what you're talking about," I said, genuinely admiring her expertise.

"Well, I should hope so." Traola grinned, looking pleased by the compliment. "I've been learning and practising healing techniques for a few years now – not because someone told me I was special enough to be a healer, but because I wanted to be useful to my community."

"And the Sun Society taught you?"

"The Sun Society is teaching me," Traola corrected, her expression growing more serious and thoughtful. "That's the thing about their approach – learning never really stops. Every case is different, every situation teaches you something new. It's much more dynamic than the traditional model where you study for a few years, get certified, and then just repeat the same techniques forever."

This sounded exactly like the kind of flexible, practical approach that my situation needed. "How long have you been with them?"

"About three years." Something darker flickered across her face. "I came from a village not too different from yours, actually. We had one official healer who was getting old and cranky, and no one was allowed to learn any healing skills – just basic first aid as a bit of backup. They said it would 'interfere with proper authority'. When he died suddenly, half the village was wiped out in the epidemic that followed – no one else knew how to treat serious illnesses."

"That's awful." My heart clenched with sympathy, seeing the pain in her eyes.

"It was completely preventable." Traola's voice was taut with old frustration and grief, her hands clenching briefly on the table. "That's when I decided the traditional system was not just flawed but actively dangerous. I left to find a better way, and that's when I found the Sun Society."

"Do you ever regret leaving?" I asked softly.

Traola considered this seriously, her gaze distant for a moment. "I miss some of the people, and I miss the familiarity of home. But I don't regret learning skills that actually help people, and I don't regret being part of a community that values practical results over pointless hierarchy." She looked back at me, and the intensity in her eyes made my breath catch. "Some things are worth leaving home for."

We talked late into the evening. I told her about Miltoven's small size, about how everyone knew everyone else's business. I told her about Nikola, how he worked at the tavern, how he couldn't come with me because of his elderly parents. Traola nodded sympathetically but didn't press for details, seeming to understand instinctively what I was willing to share.

I found myself genuinely liking Traola – perhaps more than was entirely comfortable. She was funny, smart, and refreshingly direct about the world's problems without being cynical about the possibility of solutions. More importantly, she seemed to understand exactly what I was going through. Every time she laughed, I felt an answering warmth in my chest that I kept trying to ignore. This was just admiration, I told myself. Just gratitude for finding help. Nothing more.

"The hardest part," Traola said as we finally prepared to retire for the night, her voice softer now in the quieter tavern, "is accepting that you've been lied to about your own capabilities. Not maliciously, necessarily, but lied to all the same. You've been told that magic is dangerous and complicated and should only be practised by experts, when the truth is that it's just as natural as breathing for most elves."

"But what if I'm no good at it?" I asked, voicing the fear that had been lurking at the back of my mind since Grandmother Holda first suggested this path.

"Then you'll get better with practice." Traola said it simply, as if it were the most obvious thing in the world. "That's how learning works. The Sun Society doesn't expect anyone to be perfect immediately – they expect them to be willing to try, willing to learn from mistakes, and willing to help others do the same." She stood, stretching, and I tried not to notice the lean lines of her body, the way her shirt pulled across her shoulders. "Get some rest. Tomorrow's going to be a long day of travel, but it'll be worth it. I promise."

"Thank you," I said, meaning it more than she could know.

# Chapter Six

After a day's travel and a night spent beneath the stars – where I'd lain awake for hours listening to Traola's steady breathing from across our small campfire, trying not to think about how close she was – the next morning dawned clear and cool, perfect weather for approaching Thornwood Forest.

"Ready to have your worldview thoroughly scrambled?" she asked as we saddled our horses. Her hair was even more dishevelled than usual, and there was a leaf caught in one of her curls that I had to resist the urge to pluck out.

"I think my worldview has already been fairly well scrambled," I replied. "At this point, I'm just hoping to put the pieces back together in a way that actually helps my father."

"Oh, we can definitely do that." Traola said it with the kind of confidence that suggested she'd seen it happen many times before. "The Sun Society specialises in helping people put their worldviews back together in more useful configurations."

We rode east towards the forest, following a path that gradually grew less defined as we moved away from the main travel routes. The trees grew taller and more densely packed, their branches weaving together overhead to filter the sunlight into a green-gold glow that made everything feel slightly magical. The air grew cooler, damper, rich with the scent of moss and earth and growing things. Bird calls echoed through the canopy, and occasionally I'd catch glimpses of small animals darting through the undergrowth.

"Tell me more about how the Sun Society actually works," I said as we navigated around a fallen log, moss-covered and half-rotted, already being reclaimed by the forest. "I understand the philosophy, but what does daily life look like?"

"Much more relaxed than you might expect." Traola's voice carried easily through the quiet forest. "We don't have the rigid hierarchies and formal rules that most communities rely on. Instead, we have a lot of informal co-operation and shared responsibility."

"That sounds chaotic." I tried to imagine Miltoven operating that way and couldn't.

"It can be, sometimes," Traola admitted cheerfully, turning in her saddle to grin at me. "But it's also incredibly flexible. When someone has a problem, the whole community tries to come up with solutions instead of waiting for a designated authority figure to make a decision. It's faster, more creative, and usually more effective."

We rode in comfortable silence for a while, and I found myself watching the way Traola moved with her horse – completely at ease, as if they were one creature rather than two. The forest sounds surrounded us: the rustle of leaves, the distant call of a jay, the steady rhythm of hoofbeats on soft earth. I found myself relaxing for the first time in weeks, the constant knot of anxiety in my chest loosening slightly. There was something about being surrounded by trees and moving towards a solution that made me feel more optimistic about everything.

"Can I ask you something?" I said eventually, breaking the peaceful silence.

"Of course."

"What made you decide to trust me so quickly? For all you know, I could be a spy from the Healers' Guild or someone looking to cause trouble."

Traola laughed, the sound bright and unguarded. "A spy from the Healers' Guild would never admit to having problems with an official healer. They'd have some elaborate cover story about doing research or investigating alternative methods. You, on the other hand, told me exactly what your problem is and asked for help in the most straightforward way possible."

"That's it?" It seemed almost too simple.

"That, and you have the look of someone who's genuinely desperate rather than someone who's playing games." Traola glanced back at me, her expression more serious now. "Trust me. You develop an eye for the difference when you've lived in a community that attracts both sincere seekers and troublemakers."

We stopped for lunch beside a small stream. I dismounted gratefully, my legs stiff from hours in the saddle. Traola showed me how to identify several edible plants that grew wild along the streambank, kneeling in the soft earth with unselfconscious ease. It was the kind of practical knowledge that I'd never thought to learn, since my village had always emphasised staying within prescribed roles rather than developing diverse skills.

"This is wild garlic," Traola said, pointing to a cluster of green shoots with distinctive pointed leaves. She broke one off and held it up to my nose. The sharp, pungent smell made my eyes water slightly. "Excellent for cooking, and it has natural antibiotic properties."

"That's amazing." I was genuinely impressed, watching as she identified plant after plant with easy confidence. "You know your stuff."

"The Sun Society believes in understanding your environment." Traola stood, brushing dirt from her knees, and I noticed grass stains on her trousers that matched the ones now on mine. "We don't just live in the forest – we work with it. The more you know about the plants and animals around you, the better equipped you are to take care of yourself and your community."

As we continued deeper into the forest after lunch, I began to notice signs of elven habitation: small clearings showing evidence of recent use, with neatly stacked firewood and carefully tended herb gardens. Fruit trees that had clearly been planted rather than growing wild, their branches heavy with ripening apples and pears. Delicate wind chimes hanging from the branches, crafted from shells and small bells, tinkling softly in the gentle breeze. The sound was ethereal, otherworldly.

"We're getting close," Traola said, noticing my observations. There was warmth in her voice, the pride of someone coming home. "The settlement is just ahead."

A wave of nervousness hit me with full force, sudden and overwhelming. My hands tightened on Copper's reins, and my stomach churned with anxiety. Very soon, I would meet the Sun Society and find out whether they were willing to help me learn the skills I needed to save Father. Everything hinged on me making a good first impression. What if I said the wrong thing? What if they saw through me and decided I wasn't worthy of their knowledge?

"Traola," I said, my voice coming out smaller than I'd intended, "what if they don't like me?"

"Then they have terrible judgement." Traola said it without hesitation, turning to look at me with such conviction that I almost believed her. "But honestly, I'm not worried. You're exactly the kind of person they enjoy working with."

"What kind of person is that?" I needed to hear it, needed the reassurance.

"Someone who cares more about solving problems than following rules." Traola's eyes held mine, steady and sure. "Someone who's willing to question authority when it isn't working. Someone who puts family loyalty above the convenience of following society's expectations."

The words warmed something in my chest, easing the knot of fear. Before I could respond, we crested a small hill, and the Sun Society settlement spread out below us.

My breath caught in my throat.

It was unlike any community I'd ever seen. Instead of neat rows of identical houses, the buildings here were scattered throughout the trees in a seemingly random pattern that somehow felt perfectly natural. Gardens bloomed everywhere, not just in designated areas but integrated into the landscape as if the entire settlement was one enormous, carefully tended ecosystem. I saw vegetables growing alongside wildflowers, fruit trees intermingled with ornamental plantings, herb gardens flowing naturally into the forest floor. It was chaotic and beautiful and utterly unlike the rigid order I'd grown up with.

Elves moved through the space with the same organic grace as the architecture. Children played games, and adults worked on various projects in small groups, their laughter and conversation drifting up to us on the breeze. A pair of elves tended a garden together, another group appeared to be building something, and near what looked like a communal cooking area, several people prepared food whilst chatting animatedly. Everyone looked genuinely happy to be there – engaged, purposeful, at ease.

"Welcome to the Sun Society," Traola said with obvious pride, her whole face alight with affection for this place. "What do you think?"

"It's beautiful." My voice came out hushed, almost reverent. "It looks like what a community would be if you started from scratch and built it to make people happy instead of to maintain order."

"Exactly." Traola's smile was radiant, pleased by my assessment. "Come on. Let me introduce you to some people."

As we rode down into the settlement, people looked up and waved at Traola with genuine warmth. She called out greetings, laughed at shouted jokes, and I watched the way she lit up even more surrounded by her community. This was where she belonged, I realised. These were her people in a way that went beyond simple geography.

I felt a growing sense of possibility mixed with trepidation. This place was so different from everything I knew. Could I fit in here, even temporarily? Could I learn what I needed to?

"You're thinking too hard," Traola said softly, her horse drawing alongside Copper. "I can practically hear your thoughts spinning. Just breathe. Be yourself. That's all they'll ask of you."

I took a deep breath, trying to calm my racing nerves. Maybe, just maybe, I had found exactly what I'd been looking for.

# Chapter Seven

The first thing I noticed about the Sun Society members I met was how relaxed they all seemed. Back in Miltoven, adults always carried themselves with a certain weight of responsibility, as if the proper functioning of civilisation depended on maintaining serious expressions and following established protocols. Every interaction was measured, careful, weighted with the consciousness of social hierarchies and proper behaviour.

Here, people laughed easily and treated every conversation like an opportunity to learn something new rather than a test of who knew the most. It was disorientating and wonderful in equal measure.

"This is Elenah," Traola announced to a group gathered around what appeared to be a community workspace – a large open area with work benches, tools, and various projects in different stages of completion. "She's looking for help with her father's lung fever."

"Welcome," said a middle-aged elf with greying hair pulled back in a practical braid. His smile was genuine, reaching the corners of his eyes. "I'm Brennan. Tell us, what brings you into our orbit?"

I found myself once again telling my story to an audience of sympathetic strangers. But unlike my previous experiences, this time my listeners kept interrupting with questions, suggestions, and occasional bursts of indignation on my family's behalf. It felt less like recounting a tragedy and more like enlisting allies in a cause.

"Wait, wait," said a young elven man with an elaborate beard and what looked like dried herbs braided into his hair. His eyes were bright with outrage. "Your local healer refused to treat your father because your mother accidentally stepped on her roses? That's terrible! I can't think of anything more ridiculous!"

"I don't know," said a woman who was weaving something colourful on a handloom, her fingers never stopping their practised movements, "remember when that merchant tried to convince us that healing magic only worked if you charged money for it? That was pretty ridiculous."

"Oh, right," the bearded man said thoughtfully, stroking his beard as if the memory pained him. "Yeah, that was pretty ridiculous too!"

I found myself laughing despite my worries. These people treated the absurdities of the wider world as entertainment rather than insurmountable problems. There was a lightness here, an ease that I'd never experienced before.

"So what's the plan?" Brennan asked. "Are we teaching her the collaborative fever-breaking technique?"

"I was thinking we'd start with basic magical theory and work up to the collaborative stuff," Traola said, and I felt a flutter of warmth at the certainty in her voice. "She's never had any training."

"No problem," the bearded man said cheerfully, grinning at me with such confidence I almost believed him. "I'm Fenris, by the way. I was formally trained at a Guild academy. I had to unlearn half of what they taught me before I could actually help anyone."

"What kind of things did you have to unlearn?" I asked, fascinated.

"Oh, all sorts of nonsense," Fenris said, settling into what was obviously a favourite topic. His eyes lit up with the passion of someone who loved to share knowledge. "They taught me that healing magic was dangerous and unpredictable, that it required years of study to use safely, and that collaboration was impossible because different people's magical energies would interfere with each other."

"And none of that was true?" My worldview was cracking further with every conversation.

"None of it," confirmed the woman with the loom, looking up from her weaving with a wry smile. "I'm Vera, by the way," she added quickly, keen to explain. "Healing magic is actually quite stable and forgiving. You can learn the basics in a few days, and collaborative techniques work better than individual efforts for most applications."

A few days. My heart hammered with hope. "Why would anyone want to teach things that aren't true?"

"Because scared people are easier to control," Brennan said bluntly, his expression darkening. "If everyone believes magic is too dangerous for ordinary people to use, then only the officially designated experts get to practise it. And if only the experts get to practise it, then the experts get to control who receives healing and under what circumstances."

This made an uncomfortable amount of sense. I thought about Healer Morvaine's petty power play and realised that it was only possible because everyone in Miltoven believed they had no alternatives. We'd been taught helplessness, and we'd accepted it as the natural order.

"So how does it actually work?" I asked. "The collaborative healing, I mean."

"Want to see a demonstration?" Traola suggested, her eyes bright with enthusiasm. "We've got a patient who could use some attention – nothing dramatic, just a sprained ankle that's taking longer to heal than it should."

"You'd let me watch?" I could hardly believe it. Back home, healing was done behind closed doors, shrouded in mystery and authority.

"Of course," Vera said, as if this was obvious. "How else would you learn?"

They led me to a small building that served as a medical area, though inside it looked more like a cosy living room. A young elf sat in one of the chairs with her foot propped up on a cushioned stool, a book open in her lap, though her expression suggested she was more bored than absorbed.

"Kira, meet Elenah," Traola said. "She's learning collaborative healing. Mind if we use your ankle for educational purposes?"

"Finally," Kira said with dramatic relief, closing her book with a snap. "I was starting to think you'd all forgotten about me."

"We would never forget about you," Fenris said solemnly, though his eyes sparkled with humour. "You're too entertaining to forget."

"Flatterer," Kira replied, but she was smiling, clearly pleased.

I watched as Brennan, Fenris, Vera, and Traola arranged themselves around Kira's chair, explaining what they were doing as they went. My pulse quickened with anticipation and nervousness. This was it – I was about to see real collaborative magic, the kind the Healers' Guild claimed was impossible.

"The key to collaborative healing," Traola said, positioning herself near Kira's injured ankle, "is not trying to impose your will on the injury. Instead, you work with the body's natural healing processes to encourage and accelerate them."

"Each person contributes a different aspect," Vera added, settling into position on the opposite side. "I'm focusing on reducing inflammation, Fenris is encouraging tissue repair, Brennan is managing pain, and Traola is co-ordinating everything."

"For now, just observe and try to sense what we're doing," Traola said, her eyes finding mine. "Learning to feel magical energy is the first step."

They began the healing process, and I was amazed by how natural and effortless it looked. There were no dramatic gestures or mysterious incantations like I'd always imagined, just four people positioned quietly with their hands placed gently on or near Kira's injured ankle. Their faces were calm, focused but not strained. It looked almost meditative.

Even though I couldn't see anything obvious happening – no glowing lights or visible magic – I could feel something. It was like a warm, gentle current flowing between the healers and their patient, purposeful and harmonious. The air itself seemed to hum with it, and I felt goosebumps rise on my arms.

"I can feel it," I said softly, not wanting to disrupt the process.

"That's excellent," Traola murmured without opening her eyes, and I felt a swell of pride at the approval in her tone. "Try to follow the flow of energy. See if you can sense what each of us is doing."

I focused intently, closing my eyes and reaching out with senses I hadn't known I possessed. Gradually, I began to distinguish different qualities in the magical energy. Vera's contribution felt cool and soothing, like a gentle stream washing over heated skin. Fenris' was warm and encouraging, like sunlight on a spring day. Brennan's had a steady, blocking quality that seemed to absorb discomfort, creating a buffer of calm. And Traola's wove through and around the others like a conductor guiding an orchestra, co-ordinating and harmonising all the different threads into one cohesive whole.

"How does it feel, Kira?" Brennan asked after several minutes, his voice quiet and gentle.

"Much better," Kira said, flexing her foot experimentally. Her expression brightened with relief. "The pain doesn't feel so intense now. More like a dull ache instead of a sharp stabbing."

"Excellent," Traola said, stepping back with satisfaction. "That should finish healing properly over the next day or two. Just take it easy, don't push it."

I stared at them all in amazement. "That was incredible. It looked so easy."

"It is easy, once you know how," Fenris said, his grin infectious. "The hard part is convincing people that it doesn't have to be difficult and mysterious."

"Could I really learn to do that?" I asked, hardly daring to hope.

"You could learn to do that this week," Vera said confidently, as if she were stating an obvious fact. "Your father's condition is more complex than a sprained ankle, but the basic principles are the same."

"This week?" I felt a surge of hope mixed with disbelief. It seemed impossible. "Really?"

"Really," Traola confirmed, and the warmth in her eyes made my chest tighten. "We'll start with simple exercises to help you connect with your natural magical abilities, then move on to basic healing techniques, and finish with collaborative methods for treating serious illnesses."

"And you think that will be enough to help my father?" I couldn't keep the desperate hope out of my voice.

"I think that will be enough to give you options," Brennan said diplomatically, his expression gentle but honest. "Which is really all anyone can ask for."

***

As evening approached, Traola showed me to a guest cottage – a small, charming building nestled between two ancient oaks. The interior was simple but comfortable, with a bed covered in a patchwork quilt and a small table and chair near the window.

After arranging the plush pillows on the bed to my liking, I let out a slow breath, still half in disbelief at how welcoming everyone had been. No suspicion, no interrogation, no demands for payment or proof of worthiness. Just open-handed generosity. Traola leant against the doorway, watching me with a smile that was equal parts warmth and mischief, and I felt that now-familiar flutter in my chest.

"You've had a long day," she said, her voice soft. "If you'd rather rest, no one would fault you. But if you've got a little energy left, I could give you a quick tour. Nothing too demanding – just enough so you don't wake up tomorrow completely lost."

I straightened, touched by her thoughtfulness. After the guarded suspicion I'd grown up with in Miltoven, this open generosity still felt strange, almost fragile, as if I might wake to find it gone.

I shook my head without hesitation. "I'd be honoured to go with you."

Traola's grin widened, and I noticed the way it made her eyes crinkle at the corners, the way it transformed her entire face. "Good. Follow me."

As we walked, I tried to focus on memorising the layout of the settlement rather than on how close she was walking beside me or how her shoulder occasionally brushed against mine on the narrow paths.

She was just being kind, I told myself firmly. This was how she probably treated everyone

– with this generous warmth, this easy companionship. It didn't mean anything special. She was a naturally caring person, someone who'd dedicated herself to helping others. Of course she would be lovely to me. It was her way, her nature.

But when she laughed at something I said, or when her hand briefly touched my arm to guide me around an exposed root, I felt that traitorous flutter again. It was just gratitude, I reasoned. She was willing to help me save Father's life. Anyone would feel drawn to someone offering such incredible kindness. It was natural to feel this gravitation towards her, this pull. It didn't mean anything more than appreciation for her help.

I thought of Nikola. I missed him. I loved him. This thing I was feeling for Traola was just... what? Admiration? Gratitude? The intoxication of being somewhere so different, so liberating?

Yes, that was it. I was just grateful, just overwhelmed by kindness after days of stress and worry. There was nothing more to it than that.

Even as I told myself this, I couldn't help noticing the way the fading light caught in Traola's auburn curls, or the unconscious grace with which she moved through her beloved forest home.

I pushed the thoughts away. My priority was Father. Everything else – including these confusing, inconvenient feelings – could wait.

# Chapter Eight

Traola led me down a path that wound through the heart of the settlement, past gardens that blended effortlessly into the forest. The evening air was cool and sweet with the scent of pine and wild herbs. At first, everything looked permanent, almost idyllic – a hidden village that had grown organically from the forest floor. But as we walked, I began to notice small details that suggested the Sun Society lived far more lightly and flexibly than I had assumed.

"Those buildings," I said, pausing to examine a structure that looked substantial but somehow temporary. The joints were clever, designed to come apart. "They're not permanent, are they?"

"Very observant," Traola said with approval. "Most of our structures can be taken apart and reassembled elsewhere. We've learnt to live lightly on the land."

"Why?"

"Several reasons," Traola said, settling onto a fallen log and patting the space beside her. I sat, careful to maintain a respectable distance even as I was acutely aware of her nearness. "First, it's better for the forest – we don't want to permanently alter the landscape. Second, it gives us flexibility if we need to move quickly. And third, it reflects our philosophy about not getting too attached to any particular way of doing things."

As if summoned by our conversation, an older elf approached us with what looked like a partially disassembled chair in his arms. His clothes were practical and well-worn, marked by years of honest labour, and he moved with the easy confidence of someone comfortable with physical work. His hair was silver-grey, pulled back in a simple tail, and his face was weathered but kind.

"Ah, perfect timing," Traola said, brightening. "Elenah, meet Caelen. He's one of our master builders and the person who taught me most of what I know about living sustainably."

"Pleasure to meet you," Caelen said, setting down his chair parts and extending a callused hand. His grip was firm. "I've heard about your situation. I hope we can help."

"Everyone here seems so willing to help strangers," I observed, still marvelling at it. "Is that part of your philosophy too?"

"It's part of being nomadic," Caelen explained, settling onto another log across from us. "When you move around regularly, you never know when you might need help from people you've never met before. So – after getting past the usual suspicions and cautions – we try to treat every stranger like someone we might depend on someday."

"Nomadic…" I said the word slowly, testing it. "You don't stay in one place?"

"Not permanently," Traola said. "This settlement has been here for about two years, but before that we were in the Silverleaf Valley, and before that near the Coastal Highlands. We move every few years."

"Why?" The concept was so foreign to me I could barely grasp it. Miltoven had stood in the same place for generations. My family's cottage had been my father's father's cottage. Permanence was the foundation of everything I knew.

"Lots of reasons," Caelen said, warming to the topic. "Sometimes we've learnt everything we can from a particular environment. Sometimes it's to ensure we avoid trouble – staying in one place too long can attract unwanted attention from those who disapprove of our methods. Sometimes we just get restless and want to see new places."

"How do you decide where to go next?" The logistics seemed impossibly complicated.

"Community discussion," Traola said, her eyes bright with enthusiasm. "We talk about what we want to learn, what kind of environment would serve our goals, and what areas might benefit from our presence. Then we scout locations and make a collective decision."

"Doesn't that create chaos? All those different opinions?" I thought of Miltoven's village council meetings, which were carefully structured to prevent exactly that kind of free-for-all.

"It creates conversation," Caelen said, "which is far more interesting than having one person make all the decisions. Also, when everyone can give their input, they feel invested in making it work."

As we continued through the settlement, I saw more evidence of the Sun Society's mobile lifestyle. Tools and equipment were designed for easy transport, with handles that folded and parts that nested together. Even the most substantial-looking buildings showed signs of being assembled with mobility in mind – modular walls, removable roofs, foundations that didn't dig deep into the earth.

"This is remarkable," I said. "How long have you been living this way?"

"The Sun Society has been nomadic for about fifteen years – so quite a while before I joined," Traola said. "It started as a practical necessity – being driven out of places by those who objected to our methods – but most people discovered they actually prefer it."

"What do you like about it?" I watched her face as she considered the question, fascinated by the play of emotions across her features.

"Freedom," said a voice from behind us, and we turned to see Vera approaching. "Freedom to change our minds, freedom to explore new possibilities, freedom from the kind of accumulated possessions that tie you down to one way of life."

"Plus," Caelen added, "when you live lightly, you have to be more creative about solving problems. You can't just accumulate stuff until you have the perfect tool for every situation. You have to learn to improvise, adapt, make do with what you have."

"It's liberating," Vera said. "When you know you can handle whatever comes up with just the essentials, you stop worrying about all the things you don't have."

We made our way towards what appeared to be a central gathering area where the evening meal was being prepared. I watched in fascination as dozens of elves contributed to the effort without any apparent co-ordination or hierarchy. People moved seamlessly between tasks, laughing and chatting as they worked.

"How does everyone know what to do?" I asked, amazed by the smooth choreography of it all.

"Practice," Vera said simply. "When you eat together every day, you develop a rhythm. People gravitate towards the tasks they're good at or enjoy doing."

"And if someone doesn't pull their weight?" I thought of the complex systems of obligation and shame that governed work distribution in Miltoven.

"That becomes obvious pretty quickly in a small community," Traola said. "But we've found that when people feel valued and included, they usually want to contribute. The problems come when you try to force participation or create elaborate rules about who has to do what."

"Tell us about your village," Fenris said, appearing beside us with bowls and spoons. "What's it like living in one place all the time?"

"Stable," I said, then paused to really think about the question. No one had ever asked me to critically examine my own way of life before. "But also... limiting, I suppose. Everyone has their role, and they're expected to stay in it. People like to keep things the way they are. Maybe they're scared of change."

"Do you like it?" asked a young elven woman I hadn't met yet, her expression genuinely curious.

"I thought I did," I said honestly, the realisation settling over me. "But being here... seeing how you live... it makes me realise how many possibilities I never even considered."

"What kind of possibilities?" Caelen asked.

"The possibility that knowledge doesn't have to be hoarded by experts. That communities can function without rigid hierarchies. That you can choose to change your life instead of just accepting what you're given." I surprised myself with the passion in my voice, the way the words seemed to pour out. "Where I come from, people act like the way things are is the way things have to be. But that's not true, is it?"

"Not even close," Traola said with satisfaction. "Almost everything about how society works is just a choice that people made and keep making. If you don't like those choices, you can make different ones."

"It's wonderfully diverse," Vera added. "Different people trying different approaches, learning from each other, adapting what works and discarding what doesn't. That's much healthier than everyone doing the same thing because they're afraid to experiment."

Someone placed a steaming bowl of soup in my hands – comforting, tasty, and surprisingly restorative. The broth was rich and herbed, with tender vegetables and what tasted like wild mushrooms. It was wonderful, expertly made. I ate gratefully, but even as I savoured it, I found myself missing the soups that Nikola brought home from the tavern. Those simpler broths had their own comfort, not because they were better, but because they were tied to him – to his smile as he presented them, to the ritual of sharing a meal at our small table, to the warmth of his presence beside me. I missed him. Gods, I missed him. I wondered what he was doing tonight, whether he was thinking of me as much as I was thinking of him.

I pushed the thoughts away and focused on the conversation flowing around me. The Sun Society members asked about my village, my journey, and my thoughts on the differences between settled and nomadic life. Their questions were probing but never judgemental, genuinely curious rather than testing.

"The hardest part for newcomers," Caelen said at one point, his voice thoughtful, "is usually letting go of the need for external validation. When you live in a traditional community, your worth is determined by how well you fit into established roles. Here, your worth comes from how much you contribute to the collective wellbeing, regardless of what title or position you hold."

"Security comes from your community and your skills," Traola said. "Not from your possessions or your position in a hierarchy. When you know that your people will support you and that you have abilities that are genuinely useful, you don't need external markers of status."

"Plus," added Fenris, gesturing with his spoon, "being nomadic means you always have the option to leave if things aren't working out. That's a kind of security that settled people don't have."

As everyone prepared to retire for the night, the gathering slowly dispersing as people drifted towards their dwellings, I reflected on everything I'd observed. The Sun Society had created a way of life that seemed almost impossibly idealistic – a community without rigid rules or permanent structures, where everyone was both teacher and student, where decisions were made collectively and problems were solved through creativity rather than authority.

And yet it clearly worked. These people were healthy, happy, and productive. They'd developed innovative techniques for everything from healing to agriculture. Most importantly, they'd created a sustainable way of living that didn't depend on exploiting either the environment or each other.

"Tomorrow," Traola said as we reached my guest cottage, the structure barely visible in the deepening darkness, "we'll start your training. But I wanted you to see how we live first, so you'd understand that learning healing techniques is just part of a much larger approach to life: the principles that make collaborative healing work – sharing knowledge, trusting each other, and adapting to circumstances – are the same ones that make our whole community work. You can't really separate one from the other."

That night as I lay in bed, I found myself imagining what it might be like to live this way permanently – to wake up each morning knowing the day would bring new opportunities to learn and explore, to be part of a community that valued questions over obedience, contribution over status. Another part of me wished I could learn everything I needed to know in less than a week; I desperately wanted to get back to Father and help him, to see Nikola again, to reassure myself that they were both still there waiting for me. I knew, however, that the enormity of what the Sun Society wanted to teach me couldn't be underestimated.

# Chapter Nine

My first lesson in practical magic took place at dawn in a clearing where the morning sunlight filtered through the trees in golden streams, each beam visible in the cool mist that clung to the forest floor. Traola had explained that whilst magic could be practised anywhere, natural settings made it easier for beginners to connect with their innate abilities.

"The first thing you need to understand," she said as we settled onto cushions placed in a circle, "is that you already know how to use magic. You've been using it your whole life without realising it."

I stared at her, certain I'd misheard. "That's impossible. I've never done any magic."

"Magic isn't just spells and healing," said Fenris, who had joined us for the morning lesson, settling cross-legged with his usual easy grace. "Every time you've had a gut feeling about something that turned out to be right, every time you've felt inexplicably drawn to or repelled by a person or place, every time you've known something was wrong even when everything looked fine – that was magic."

The words sent a shiver through me. I considered this, thinking back to the times I'd just known that Father was getting worse before Mother had said anything, the way I'd always been able to sense Nikola's mood the moment I saw him. "You mean intuition?"

"Intuition is one form of magic," Traola confirmed. "So is the way some people can make plants grow better just by being around them, or the way certain individuals can calm frightened animals without saying a word. Magic is about connection and influence, not just dramatic effects."

My mind reeled. Everything I'd been taught said magic was rare, dangerous, the domain of trained experts. And yet they were telling me I'd been doing it all along?

"The reason most elves think they can't do magic," Fenris added, his voice gentle but firm, "is that they're looking for the wrong things. They expect fireworks and lightning bolts when what they should be noticing is subtlety and flow."

"So how do I learn to notice it?" My voice came out hushed, almost reverent. This felt like being told I had eyes I'd never opened, senses I'd never used.

"By paying attention to what you're already doing," Traola said, her tone soothing and encouraging. "Close your eyes and take a few deep breaths. Try to sense the life around you – not with your regular senses, but with whatever part of you knows things without being told."

I closed my eyes. At first, all I could hear was the normal sound of the forest: birds calling their morning songs, leaves rustling in the gentle breeze, the distant burble of a stream. I tried to focus, to reach for something more, but the harder I tried, the more elusive it became.

Then I remembered what Traola had said. Stop trying so hard. Just pay attention.

I relaxed, letting my breathing slow, releasing the tension in my shoulders. And suddenly, gradually, like dawn breaking, I began to sense something else – a kind of gentle humming energy that seemed to come from everywhere all at once. It was in the trees, in the earth beneath me, in the very air. Alive. Singing. Present.

"I think I feel something," I said tentatively, afraid that speaking would break the spell.

"Describe it," Traola encouraged.

"It's like... like everything is quietly singing?" I struggled to find words for the sensation, frustrated by how inadequate language felt. "Not actual singing, but something that feels musical and alive. Like the whole world is humming with energy."

"That's exactly it," Fenris confirmed. "That's the magical energy that flows through all living things. The more you practise sensing it, the easier it becomes to work with it."

I opened my eyes, and the world looked different. Not visibly changed, but I was aware of it in a way I'd never been before.

Every tree, every blade of grass, every insect – all of it was alive with this singing energy. How had I never noticed it before? How had I lived twenty-three years blind to something so fundamental?

We spent the morning teaching me simple exercises to strengthen my awareness of magical energy, and each new discovery felt like a revelation. I learnt to sense the difference between healthy plants and stressed ones – the healthy ones sang clear and strong whilst the struggling ones had a discordant, muffled quality. I felt the emotional states of nearby animals – a rabbit's nervous alertness, a bird's contentment as it preened in the sun. I detected the subtle energy patterns that surrounded other people – Traola's energy was warm and steady like a banked fire, whilst Fenris' was quicker, more playful, like dancing flames.

"Illness and injury create disturbances in the normal flow of magical energy," Traola explained, watching as I practised sensing a nearby grove of trees. "If you can sense those disturbances, you can work to correct them."

"Show me," I said, barely able to contain my eagerness. This was real. This was actually happening. I was learning to do things I'd been told my entire life were beyond me.

Traola picked up a flower with bruised petals and a bent stem, handling it with careful reverence. "Put your hands near the flower and try to sense it," she instructed.

I held my hands a few inches from the flower and closed my eyes, focusing my attention the way they'd taught me. Almost immediately, I could feel something was off – the flower's energy felt disrupted and uneven, like a song with missing notes, like a voice singing off-key.

"I can feel that it's hurt," I said, startled by both the flower's pain and the fact that I could sense it so clearly. "It feels... broken. Confused."

"Good. Very good." Traola's voice was soft, encouraging. "Now, instead of trying to force it to be healthy, just send it some of your own energy and imagine the disruption smoothing out. Like helping someone find the right note in a song."

I concentrated, trying to share some of my own vitality with the struggling flower. It felt natural, instinctive – like offering my hand to someone who'd stumbled. To my amazement, I could actually feel the plant's energy beginning to stabilise and strengthen, its song growing clearer and more harmonious.

"Open your eyes," Traola said quietly.

I looked down at the flower and gasped, my hand flying to my mouth. The bruised petals had regained their colour – not completely, but visibly improved, the purple marks fading to pale shadows. The bent stem had straightened, standing proud once more. It wasn't perfectly healed, but the transformation was undeniable.

"That was me?" I whispered, half in awe, half in disbelief. My hands were trembling. "I did that?"

"You did that," Fenris reassured me. "And if you can heal a flower, you can heal a person. The principles are exactly the same."

"But my father's illness is much more serious than a damaged flower." Fear crept back in, tempering my excitement. What if this didn't scale? What if I could help flowers but not people?

"That's why we use collaborative techniques for complex cases," Traola said, her hand resting briefly on my shoulder – a grounding touch that steadied me. "One person working alone might not have enough energy to heal serious lung fever, but people working together have a much better chance."

We spent the afternoon practising on progressively more challenging subjects: a bird with a broken wing that Fenris had found near the settlement, a rabbit with a shallow cut on its hind leg, an old tree that had been damaged by lightning. Each time, I felt that same rush of wonder when I sensed the disruption in their energy, that same fierce joy when I felt them begin to heal.

The bird was the most profound. I could feel its fear and pain, could sense how the break in its wing had shattered not just bone but its confidence in flight. When Fenris and I worked together to heal it – my energy supporting and encouraging whilst his mended and repaired – I felt the moment when the bird's song returned to fullness. When we released it and it flew away, I cried openly, overwhelmed by the beauty and impossibility of what I'd just done.

"The most important thing to remember," Fenris said as we wrapped up the day's lessons, the sun beginning its descent towards the horizon, "is that you're not imposing your will on the patient. You're working with their body's natural healing processes to help them recover more quickly and completely."

"What's the difference?" I asked, wiping at my damp cheeks, not embarrassed by the tears.

"Trying to impose your will is exhausting and often counterproductive," Traola explained. "Working with natural processes is much more efficient and effective. Plus, it's safer for both the healer and the patient."

"Safer how?" Every detail felt crucial, important beyond measure.

"When you try to force healing, you risk damaging the patient or burning yourself out," Fenris said. "When you work collaboratively with the body's natural systems, the worst that can happen is that nothing improves. There's very little risk of making things worse."

That evening, I sat outside my guest cottage, practising the energy-sensing exercises I'd been taught. The sun had set, and stars were beginning to emerge in the darkening sky. I marvelled at how much my understanding of the world had changed in such a short space of time.

Everything I'd been told about magic being dangerous and difficult was evidently wrong. It was no more dangerous than gardening and no more difficult than learning to cook. The only reason people thought otherwise was that they'd been deliberately kept ignorant of their own capabilities. The injustice of it made me angry, but beneath the anger was something else – a fierce, blazing hope.

"How are you feeling about everything?" Traola asked, settling beside me with her usual easy grace.

"Overwhelmed," I admitted. "But also excited. Grateful. Awed." I laughed, the sound slightly unsteady. "I just hope that when I get home to my father, I can still do this."

"You can," Traola said firmly. "I've seen dozens of people discover their magical abilities, and you're picking it up faster than most. You have a natural sensitivity to energy."

The praise made me warm all over, and I tried not to think about whether that warmth came from the compliment itself or from who was giving it.

"Tomorrow we'll work on more advanced techniques and start practising collaborative healing," Traola said. "By the end of the week, you should have everything you need to help your father."

We sat in comfortable silence for a while, the quiet broken only by the occasional rustle of leaves. I stared ahead, allowing my thoughts to drift. I hoped Father's illness hadn't worsened, that he would hold on long enough for me to get home to him.

# Chapter Ten

The next few days passed in a blur of intensive learning that left my head spinning with new concepts and my confidence growing by leaps and bounds. The Sun Society's approach to education was unlike anything I'd experienced – instead of lecturing me about theoretical principles, they showed me practical techniques and let me learn by doing. Every mistake was treated as valuable information, every success as evidence of what I'd been capable of all along.

They'd arranged for me to work with a rotating group of volunteers who had various minor ailments – headaches, muscle tension, small cuts that were healing slowly. Each session taught me something new about how magical energy flowed between people and how to adjust my contribution to complement what others were doing. It was like learning to harmonise in a song, finding the exact note that would blend with the others.

"I'm still amazed by how natural this feels," I said after successfully helping to relieve someone's back pain. The woman had stood up with tears of gratitude, and I'd felt a surge of purpose so powerful it had made me dizzy. "Why isn't everyone taught to do this?"

"Because knowledge is power," Brennan said bluntly, "and some people prefer to keep power concentrated in a few hands rather than distributed amongst many."

"But that's so wasteful," I said. "Think of all the suffering that could be prevented if everyone had these skills."

"Exactly," said Fenris. "Which is why the Sun Society exists. We're not just teaching healing methods – we're demonstrating that the whole system of artificial scarcity around magical knowledge is unnecessary."

"Artificial scarcity?" I repeated, the term unfamiliar.

"The idea that only a few special people can be trusted with important knowledge or abilities," Vera explained. "It's a way of maintaining social hierarchies by convincing people they're not capable of taking care of themselves."

I thought about Miltoven and how dependent everyone was on Healer Morvaine. How we all simply accepted that she was the only one who could help us, that we had no choice but to submit to her whims. "So you're saying that my village's entire medical system is designed to keep people helpless?"

"Perhaps not maliciously designed," Traola said carefully, "but certainly designed in a way that concentrates power and makes people dependent on a single authority figure, which inevitably leads to situations like what's happening with your father."

"What would happen if I went back to Miltoven and taught other people these techniques?" I asked, the idea taking root in my mind.

The Sun Society members exchanged meaningful looks that I couldn't quite interpret.

"That's entirely up to you," Fenris said diplomatically. "But you should be aware that introducing new ideas to an established order can be... challenging."

"Challenging how?" I asked apprehensively.

"People don't always appreciate finding out they've been unnecessarily limiting themselves," Vera said gently. "It can make them feel foolish or angry or both."

"And Healer Morvaine probably wouldn't be thrilled about competition," Traola added, her expression darkening. "People whose authority depends on artificial scarcity tend to react poorly when that scarcity is threatened."

I considered this soberly. I'd been so focused on learning skills to help Father that I hadn't really thought about the broader implications of what I was doing. But now I realised that by questioning the established medical hierarchy, I was essentially challenging the entire social order of my village.

"Have other people who learnt here faced problems when they went home?" I asked.

"Some have," Brennan admitted. "Nothing dangerous, usually, but social pressure, economic retaliation, that sort of thing. People can be surprisingly vicious when they feel their worldview is being threatened."

"On the other hand," Fenris said optimistically, "we've also seen communities embrace new approaches once they see the results. It really depends on the specific situation and how you present the information."

"What's the best way to present it?"

"Focus on practical benefits rather than philosophical arguments," Vera said. "Show people that these techniques work – don't lecture them about why their old methods are wrong."

"And start small," Traola added. "Help a few people quietly, let word spread naturally, and let the results speak for themselves."

"That's assuming Bng you decide you want to do any of that," Fenris said kindly. "You're under no obligation to become a revolutionary just because you learnt some useful skills."

But even as he said it, I realised that I was already thinking like a revolutionary. The idea of going back to Miltoven and quietly accepting the status quo seemed impossible now that I knew how much unnecessary suffering it caused. How could I unsee what I'd seen? How could I unknow what I now knew?

"I think," I said slowly, "in the long run, I'm going to have some difficult decisions to make."

"Well," Traola said pragmatically, "first things first. Let's make sure you're ready to help your father. Tomorrow we're going to simulate treating someone with lung fever, using one of our members who's willing to let us create temporary symptoms."

"You can do that?" I asked in awe.

"We can simulate all the symptoms of lung fever without actually endangering anyone," Fenris explained. "It's the best way to practise treating serious conditions safely."

***

The next day, Brennan volunteered to have temporary lung fever symptoms magically induced so I could practise the techniques I'd need to help Father. My stomach churned with nervous anticipation as we gathered around him.

"This is going to feel very real," Vera warned as she prepared the spell that would simulate the illness. "Brennan will have all the symptoms of actual lung fever – difficulty breathing, fever, congestion, fatigue – but without any permanent damage."

"How long will it last?" I asked, feeling nervous about deliberately making someone unwell, even temporarily.

"Just until we cure it," Traola said reassuringly, her hand briefly touching my shoulder. "The advantage of magically-induced symptoms is that they respond very quickly to treatment."

"Ready?" Vera asked Brennan, who was reclining comfortably on a padded bench.

"Ready," he replied stoically. "Try not to make it too unpleasant."

As Vera began the spell, I watched in fascination and horror as Brennan's condition deteriorated before my eyes. His breathing grew laboured, each inhalation a struggle. His skin took on a greyish pallor and he coughed – deep, rattling coughs just like Father's worst episodes.

"That's disturbingly realistic," I said.

"It has to be," Fenris explained gently, "or the practise wouldn't be useful. Now, let's get to work."

The healing team consisted of me, Traola, Fenris, and a fourth member named Myandol, who was eager to gain experience in this area. We positioned ourselves around Brennan, and I tried to calm my racing nerves.

"Remember," Traola said softly, her voice grounding me, "don't try to force anything. Just contribute your energy to the overall aim and trust the process."

I closed my eyes and reached out with my magical senses, feeling for the disruptions in Brennan's energy that indicated illness. I could sense the inflammation in his lungs – hot and angry and wrong. The fever throwing off his body's natural rhythms like a discordant note. The overall weakness that came from fighting infection, making his whole energy field feel thin and fragile.

Using the techniques I'd learnt, I began contributing my energy to the healing effort, focusing specifically on supporting Brennan's immune response. Around me, I could feel the others working on different aspects: Fenris reducing inflammation with his warm, encouraging energy; Myandol clearing congestion with a cool, flowing sensation; and Traola co-ordinating everything, her presence steady and sure at the centre of it all.

As we worked, I could feel Brennan's condition steadily improving. His breathing became easier, the rasping wheeze smoothing out. His fever broke, and I felt the moment it happened – like clouds parting to let sun through. The greyish pallor faded from his skin, replaced by healthy colour.

"How do you feel?" Myandol asked after we'd finished.

"Completely normal," Brennan said, sitting up and taking a deep breath – full and clear and easy. "Maybe even better than normal. That was quite an experience."

"How did I do?" I asked anxiously, trembling slightly from the effort.

"You were brilliant," Traola said. "Your energy contribution was steady and well-focused. I could feel your input making a real difference."

"Really?" I needed to hear it again, needed the reassurance.

"Really," Fenris confirmed, grinning at me. "You've got a natural talent for this kind of work."

I felt a surge of relief and excitement so powerful it made me lightheaded. "So I could do this for my father's actual lung fever?"

"Absolutely," Vera said. "But we need to be realistic about what you might face when you return home."

"What do you mean?" I asked, though I suspected I already knew.

Brennan stood and stretched, fully recovered from the simulated illness. "Your father needs collaborative healing for the best results, but that requires other people to participate. People who might not believe it's possible, or who might be too frightened to try."

"We've encountered it before," Fenris added gently. "Someone returns home with these skills, eager to help, but they can't find anyone willing to work with them. Fear and scepticism can be powerful barriers."

Traola stood and gestured towards a nearby cottage. "Which is why we're going to give you some alternatives. Wait here a moment." She jogged off and disappeared through the cottage door, with Vera following her.

"Think of them as a bridge," Vera called back over her shoulder. "They can stabilise your father's condition, reduce his symptoms, and buy you time to either convince others to help or to treat him gradually on your own."

Within minutes, they returned carrying a woven basket filled with various bottles and pouches. Fenris had also fetched his own travelling pack from where it rested against a tree, pulling out additional supplies.

"This one," Traola said, lifting a dark green bottle from the basket, "helps clear lung congestion. Mix three drops with hot water and have him inhale the steam. It won't cure the infection, but it will make breathing easier."

"And this," Fenris added, presenting a pouch of dried leaves from his pack, "is for reducing fever. Brew it strong, add honey if you have it. It works best combined with magical energy, but it has some effect on its own."

Brennan contributed a small jar he'd been carrying in his belt pouch. "For his chest. Rub it in whilst channelling healing energy. Even if you're working alone, the combination of the herbs and your magic will have some impact."

"But remember," Vera said seriously, her expression grave, "don't think of these as your first choice. Your father's condition sounds severe enough that he really needs the full collaborative approach."

"I understand," I said, carefully placing each item in my pack. "But how do I convince people who've been taught their whole lives that only official healers can use magic?"

"Start with people who trust you," Myandol suggested. "Family members, close friends. Show them small demonstrations first – healing a cut or soothing a headache. Build their confidence gradually."

"And if they're still too afraid?" I asked, the fear creeping back in.

"Then you use what we're giving you and do the best you can alone," Traola said honestly. "It won't be ideal, but it will be better than nothing. These items, combined with your newly developed abilities, should at least stabilise his condition."

"The most important thing," Brennan added, "is not to exhaust yourself trying to do everything alone. Healing serious illness solo is possible but draining. Pace yourself, take breaks, and don't be afraid to stretch the treatment over multiple sessions."

Vera reached into the basket one final time and produced a bottle filled with a golden liquid that seemed to glow faintly in the dappled sunlight. "This is the most precious thing we're giving you. It's a concentrated healing elixir that we make communally, infused with the combined magical energy of our entire settlement. Use it only if nothing else is working. Three drops under the tongue, no more."

I held the bottle reverently, feeling the warmth of it against my palm, the gentle hum of power contained within. "Thank you. All of you. I can't tell you how grateful I am."

***

That afternoon, I began preparing for my journey home. I felt confident in my new abilities but also nervous about putting them to the test in a real-life situation with genuinely high stakes. Everything I'd practised here had been controlled, safe, reversible. What if I failed when it truly mattered?

"Are you ready for this?" Traola asked, joining me in the doorway of the guest cottage.

"I think so," I said, folding my cloak with careful precision. "At least, I'm as ready as I can be. Thank you for everything you've taught me."

"Thank you for trusting us," Traola said, her eyes warm. "It's been a pleasure teaching you."

"Do you think you'll want to share our techniques with your own community?" Fenris asked, joining us.

"I don't know yet," I admitted, pausing in my packing. "I don't want to upset anyone, but I can't see the sense in withholding information that could help people in their moment of need."

"Well," Vera said with a smile, appearing with a bundle of food for my journey, "you know where we are if you want to send others here for training."

***

That evening, I said my goodbyes to everyone. They had become more than acquaintances – they were friends. Real friends who'd seen me at my most uncertain and helped me discover strength I didn't know I had. A pang of sadness hit me at having to leave such a supportive, forward-thinking community, but I was eager to return home and help Father. And to see Nikola again – to feel his arms around me and hear his voice and remember what home felt like.

"Before you go," Traola said, "there's one more thing I want to show you." She led me to a high point overlooking the settlement, where we could see the entire community spread out below us in the fading light. The cottages glowed with lamplight, smoke rising from cooking fires, the sound of laughter and conversation drifting up to us.

"What do you see?" she asked.

"People living the way they choose to," I said after a moment, my voice thick with emotion. "Free from imposed limitations, working together to solve problems, creating something beautiful and sustainable."

"Good," she said. "Hold on to that, Elenah. Don't waste your potential in a village too frightened to see its people thrive."

We stood in comfortable silence for a moment, the quiet settling between us like a shared understanding. I watched as a light breeze stirred the canopy of leaves, my thoughts turning over everything I'd learnt.

"If things don't work out the way you hope," Traola began, her voice soft, "or if you decide you want to see more of the world before settling down, you'd be welcome to travel with us for a while."

"You'd really let me join you?" I asked, turning to face her, touched by the invitation.

Traola smiled, and in the fading light, she looked almost ethereal – beautiful and wild and utterly herself. "Of course. You've got a good heart, a sharp mind, and a desire to learn. It's been a pleasure having you here."

Something in my chest cracked open then. I looked at her – really looked at her – and felt overwhelmed by how much I admired this woman. How much I'd come to value her opinion, her presence, her fierce commitment to helping others. She'd shown me what was possible, had believed in me when I didn't believe in myself, had opened doors I didn't even know existed.

And I was leaving. Tomorrow, I would ride away from here, with no way of knowing if I'd ever see her again.

The thought made my eyes burn with unshed tears. Before I could think better of it, before I could talk myself out of it, I leant in towards her.

For a heartbeat, Traola leant in too. I could see her eyes widening slightly, feel the warmth of her breath, sense the magnetic pull between us. Our faces were inches apart, and then...

Traola pulled back, her hand coming up gently but firmly to create space between us.

"Elenah," she said softly, and there was so much tenderness in her voice that it made my chest ache. "I can't."

Shame flooded through me, hot and terrible. "I'm sorry. I shouldn't have..."

"No, listen to me." Traola's hands found my shoulders, grounding me when I wanted to flee. "I have so much love and respect for you. So much admiration for who you are and who you're becoming. But I know you have a partner waiting for you at home. Someone who loves you, who you love. And I would never – *never* – want to come between you and him."

The kindness in her words, the care, somehow made it worse. Tears spilt down my cheeks. "I don't understand what I'm feeling."

"You're feeling a lot of things," Traola said gently, her thumbs brushing away my tears with infinite tenderness. "You're overwhelmed, you're scared about what comes next, you're grateful for what you've found here. It's natural to confuse those feelings with something else. But that doesn't make them what you think they are."

"You felt it too," I whispered. "Just now. I know you did."

Traola's expression was achingly sad. "What I feel doesn't matter. What matters is that you go home to the person who's been waiting for you, and you don't carry guilt or confusion with you. You deserve better than that. He deserves better than that."

I closed my eyes, fresh tears leaking out. She

was right. Of course she was right. Nikola had been nothing but loyal, nothing but loving, and here I was on a hillside with another woman, trying to kiss her because I was overwhelmed and frightened and didn't know how to process everything I was feeling.

"I'm sorry," I said again, my voice breaking.

"Don't be sorry for having emotions," Traola said firmly. "Be honest about them. With yourself, and eventually with him. But don't let a moment of confusion define you or ruin something good."

She pulled me into a hug then – firm and warm and completely platonic – and I cried into her shoulder whilst she held me. When I finally pulled back, wiping at my face with my sleeves, she smiled at me with such genuine affection that it made my heart hurt in a different way.

"You're going to be fine," she said. "You're going home for your father, and you're going to work out what you want, and you're going to be fine."

***

That night, as I lay in bed, I let the sounds of the settlement lull me towards sleep. The journey home would be long, and I needed rest. Ahead lay a road that would demand every ounce of strength and clarity I could summon.

# Chapter Eleven

I left the Sun Society settlement at first light, my bags abundant with supplies and my head full of new knowledge. Traola had offered to accompany me partway home, but I'd decided I needed to make this journey alone. I needed time to think, to process everything that had happened, to prepare myself for what lay ahead.

The presence of the carefully packed blends felt like hope itself pressed against Copper's flanks. It represented Father's chance at life. I found myself checking everything obsessively, my hand reaching back to touch the bags, to reassure myself that the precious cargo was still there, that it hadn't somehow disappeared if I wasn't vigilant.

The first day of travel passed peacefully, giving me plenty of opportunity to review the healing techniques in my mind and plan how

I would approach Father's treatment. If people were too frightened or sceptical to help, I could at least stabilise Father's condition with what the Sun Society had given me whilst I worked to convince them. I practised the energy-sensing exercises whilst riding, feeling for the life force of the plants and animals around me, keeping my newly awakened magical senses sharp and ready.

As evening approached on my second day, I'd settled into a rhythm of confident urgency. Every mile brought me closer to home. I was so absorbed in hopeful thoughts that I almost didn't hear the sound of horses approaching from behind. When I finally looked back, four riders were already close, moving faster than normal travel would require.

Something about their approach made my skin prickle with unease. These weren't merchants or fellow travellers – their formation was too precise, their pace too purposeful. I guided Copper off the main road into a grove of trees, hoping to let them pass without incident. My heart began to pound as I realised they weren't going to simply ride by.

Instead of continuing on their way, the riders turned to follow me into the grove, their horses moving with the disciplined co-ordination of a military unit. As they drew closer, I could see the cold determination in their faces, and my mouth went dry with sudden fear.

"Good evening, miss," called the lead rider, a stern-looking elf with the kind of rigid posture that suggested military or official training. His voice carried the false courtesy of someone accustomed to being obeyed without question. "We'd like a word with you."

I tried desperately to keep my voice calm. "Can I help you with something?"

The leader's eyes were pale and calculating, scanning my appearance with the thoroughness of a predator evaluating prey. "We understand you've been visiting certain... unsavoury elements in the area," he said, his tone making it clear that this was an accusation rather than a casual enquiry.

"I'm not sure what you mean," I replied, though I could feel my cheeks burning with what was probably a telltale blush. My hands tightened on Copper's reins as the four riders arranged themselves in a loose circle around me, cutting off any possibility of escape.

"The Sun Society," said one of the other riders, a sharp-faced elven woman with an official-looking badge pinned to her cloak. Her voice dripped with disgust. "That den of anarchists and malcontents who think they can ignore the natural order of society."

"Don't play games with us, girl," the leader added, his false courtesy slipping away. "We've been tracking people who associate with that group of dangerous radicals. You were seen leaving their settlement, loaded down with their contraband."

I realised I was in serious trouble. These people were clearly opposed to the Sun Society with an intensity that bordered on fanatical. The way they spoke about the gentle, helpful community I'd just left made my blood run cold.

"What do you want from me?" I asked, trying to keep the tremor out of my voice and failing.

"We want to know what poison they've been filling your head with," the leader said, his horse stepping closer to mine in a deliberate intimidation tactic. "And we want you to hand over any materials they gave you. Immediately."

"I don't have any materials," I lied, acutely aware of the precious blends in my possession – the dark green bottle for lung congestion, the fever-reducing herbs, the chest blend Brennan had contributed, and most precious of all, the golden elixir that represented my last hope if all else failed. They could mean the difference between life and death for Father. I couldn't let them take...

"Search her," the woman ordered with vicious satisfaction.

"No!" I cried out, trying to pull Copper away, but the third rider had already dismounted and was reaching for my bags with rough hands. "Please, those are just... my father is dying!"

"Your father should have consulted a proper healer," the woman said coldly, "instead of sending his daughter to consort with criminals and seditionists."

Two of the riders had dismounted now and were grabbing at Copper's tack. I tried to hold the bags away from them, but one of them yanked so hard I nearly fell from the saddle. Copper whinnied in distress, sensing my panic, dancing sideways as I struggled to keep my seat.

"Stop it! Please!" My voice broke as their hands tore through my belongings, pulling out the carefully wrapped bottles and pouches with deliberate roughness.

"Look at this," one of them said triumphantly, holding up the bottle of lung congestion blend that Traola had so carefully explained. "Unauthorised magical materials. Probably dangerous to anyone foolish enough to use them."

"They're just herbal!" I said desperately. "There's nothing dangerous about them! Please, my father needs those – he's been sick for weeks, he's dying!"

The fourth rider grabbed my arm, his fingers

digging in hard enough to bruise. "Get down," he ordered, and when I didn't move fast enough, he pulled. I tumbled from Copper's back, hitting the ground hard enough to knock the wind from my lungs. Pain shot through my shoulder and hip.

"Herbs enhanced with unlicensed magic," the leader corrected, looking down at me with contempt as I struggled to catch my breath. "Contaminated with the perverted techniques of people who think they know better than centuries of established tradition. Which makes them illegal to possess without proper authorisation."

I pushed myself up on trembling arms, gasping. "Illegal according to who?" The question came out choked, desperate. "Since when do people need authorisation to carry..."

The woman kicked dirt at me, making me flinch and shield my face. "Shut your mouth, girl. You don't get to question us."

I watched in horror from the ground as they continued rifling through my bags, handling my precious supplies with casual cruelty. The chest blend disappeared into their saddlebag. The fever-reducing herbs followed. Each loss felt like a physical blow.

"Since when is it illegal to help someone who's sick?" I managed to say.

"Since the Healers' Guild established proper regulations for magical practice to protect innocent people from exactly this kind of dangerous experimentation," the woman said, her face twisted with fanatic conviction. "These Sun Society anarchists think they can ignore official procedures, but someone has to maintain order. Someone has to protect society from their reckless ideology."

"Their ideology?" I stared up at them, still on the ground, shaking with fear and rage and grief. Then I saw one of them pull out the golden elixir. "No, please, not that one..."

The rider held it up to the light, examining it with casual interest. "What's this? Some kind of poison?"

I scrambled to my feet, reaching for it. "Please, it's the only thing that might..."

He tossed it carelessly to another rider, who

caught it with a laugh. They were playing with it, with Father's last hope, like it was a toy. The golden liquid sloshed inside the bottle, and I felt something break inside me.

"Give it back!" I lunged forward, but the woman shoved me hard in the chest. I stumbled backward, my feet catching on a root, and fell again. This time my head struck something – a rock, a branch – and stars burst across my vision.

"Their ideology is helping people!" I sobbed from the ground, tasting blood in my mouth where I'd bitten my tongue. "Teaching people to take care of each other! How is that dangerous?"

"Because," the leader said with the patience of someone explaining something obvious to a petulant child, "when every ignorant peasant thinks they can practise magic, people die. When official authority is undermined by amateur practitioners, chaos follows. The Sun Society preaches the lie that knowledge belongs to everyone, when any civilised person knows that power must be carefully controlled by those qualified to wield it."

I watched through blurred vision as they carelessly stuffed the golden elixir into their collection bag.

"They're seditionists," the woman repeated, her voice rising with passionate hatred. "They deliberately undermine the proper order of society. They teach people to question legitimate authority, to reject their proper places, to think they can just... just change the way things work because they don't like the rules."

The fourth rider, who had been rifling through the last of my bags, spoke up with the fervour of a true believer. "They spread their poison wherever they go. Entire communities have been corrupted by their teachings. People abandoning their proper roles, challenging established healers, thinking they can just... decide for themselves how magic should be used."

"And look where it leads," the woman said, gesturing at me with disgust as I huddled on the ground. "Young elven women travelling alone, carrying illegal substances, thinking they know better than trained professionals. Pathetic."

I felt my world crumbling. Now I would have to quickly convince people to join me in collaborative healing. Mother would participate – I knew that with certainty. She loved Father too much to let fear stop her. And Nikola – Nikola would probably be willing too, if I asked. But the thought of asking him made my chest tighten with a different kind of fear. I couldn't bear the idea of putting him in a situation where he felt obligated to risk trouble with the Guild, where his loyalty to me might put him in a compromising position. And even then, I would still be short of enough people to help.

"Please," I begged, no longer caring about dignity or pride. I was a sobbing wreck on the ground, my clothes torn, my body aching, my hope shattered. "You don't understand. My father is dying. Our village healer won't treat him because of some petty grudge about roses. Please, I'm begging you..."

"Then you should have followed the proper channels," the leader said with stone-cold indifference, mounting his horse. "Applied to the Guild for special consideration. Requested mediation for your dispute. Worked within the system instead of running off to consort with enemies of civilised society."

"I tried the system!" I screamed up at them, my voice raw and broken. "The system failed! The system is happy to let my father die because our healer has hurt feelings about her stupid roses!"

The woman spat near my feet. "The system works when people respect it. When they don't try to circumvent proper authority the moment things become inconvenient. Your family's problems don't give you the right to associate with dangerous radicals or possess illegal substances."

I pushed myself to my knees, swaying slightly, one hand pressed to my aching head. "What about my father?" My voice came out hollow, defeated. "What am I supposed to tell him? That I found help but couldn't bring it home because someone decided helping people is illegal?"

"Tell him to petition the Guild for proper treatment," the leader said, gathering his reins. "Tell him to work within established channels. Tell him there are consequences for raising daughters who think they can ignore the law."

"Show me the law!" I shouted, anger cutting through my despair. "Show me the written statute that says carrying herbs is illegal!"

"Guild regulations have the force of law in all civilised territories," the woman said with smug certainty. "Emergency provisions for the suppression of dangerous magical practices. If you weren't an ignorant peasant corrupted by anarchist propaganda, you'd know that."

As they prepared to leave, the leader offered one final piece of advice, his voice carrying the weight of an official threat. "If I were you, girl, I'd forget everything those people taught you. The Guild has a long memory for troublemakers, and we have methods for dealing with people who persist in dangerous magical practices."

"What kind of methods?" I asked, though I wasn't sure I wanted to know.

"The kind that ensure the safety of society," the woman said with an unpleasant smile. "The kind that remind people why proper authority exists. Continue associating with the Sun Society or practising their techniques, and you'll discover just how far the Guild's reach extends."

"Your father's illness is tragic," the leader added with false sympathy that made me want to scream, "but it doesn't justify putting entire communities at risk through dangerous magical practices. Sometimes, individual suffering must be accepted for the greater good of society."

"The greater good?!" I choked out in disbelief. "You're talking about letting my father die for the greater good?"

"We're talking about maintaining the order that keeps civilisation functioning," the woman replied without a trace of compassion. "Your father is one man. The Sun Society's corruption threatens us all. Which do you think matters more?"

They rode away at a gallop, leaving me alone in the grove. I stayed on my knees for a long time, unable to move, unable to think, staring at the torn bags scattered around me. My shoulder throbbed. My head pounded.

Blood trickled from my split lip. But none of that compared to the hollow ache in my chest where hope used to be.

All my searching, learning, and preparation had been reduced to nothing by four people who thought maintaining their version of order was more important than life itself. The casual cruelty of their indifference was almost worse than their fanaticism – the way they'd hurt me, humiliated me, destroyed my last hope, all whilst believing utterly in their own righteousness.

I don't know how long I sat there. Long enough for the sun to sink lower. Long enough for the adrenaline to fade and leave me shaking uncontrollably. Long enough for the tears to stop, replaced by a vast, empty numbness.

Finally, I forced myself to stand on unsteady legs. I gathered what was left of my belongings – the torn bags, the scattered clothes, the few items they'd deemed worthless. Copper stood nearby, and when I reached for his reins, he nuzzled my shoulder gently, as if trying to comfort me.

But even as I grieved for the lost blends, even through the numbness and the pain, I felt something else growing inside me: a cold, hard determination that had nothing to do with desperation and everything to do with fury. These people had tried to steal not just Father's chance at life, but my own right to help him.

They had, however, made one crucial mistake: they'd assumed the materials were what mattered most. They'd confiscated them but left me with something much more dangerous to their cause: the unshakeable knowledge that their entire system was built on lies and maintained through cruelty.

I still had the collaborative healing techniques in my memory. I still knew how to sense and work with magical energy. I still understood the principles behind the treatments Father needed. The blends would have made things easier – they would have been my backup plan if people refused to help – but they weren't absolutely essential. I would have to work harder now, recruiting and training others despite any reluctance, but it could still be done.

As I climbed painfully back into Copper's saddle and resumed my journey home, I felt a new kind of purpose settling over me. The Guild enforcers had tried to intimidate me into compliance, to break me, to make me give up. But all they'd really done was show me exactly why the Sun Society's work was so desperately needed.

# Chapter Twelve

I approached Miltoven several days later than I'd thought it would take me, the familiar landscape both a comfort and an accusation. I'd tried to make good time – pushed Copper harder than I should have, skipped meals, slept only when exhaustion forced me to. But my body still ached from what those Guild enforcers had done to me, and twice I'd been so dizzy I'd had to stop and rest. The bruises on my shoulder and hip had turned spectacular shades of purple and yellow, and the cut on my lip had only just stopped reopening every time I tried to eat.

As the village came into view, I felt my emotions surge – relief at being home, terror at what I might find, anxiety about whether Father was even still alive. But underneath it all was a desperate, almost childish need for comfort. I couldn't go straight to my parents' cottage. Not like this, still running so high on emotion, still trembling with the aftershocks of what had happened. I couldn't let Mother see me like this – it would terrify her. And Father... Father needed hope, not the sight of his daughter barely holding herself together.

I needed Nikola. The realisation was instinctive, immediate. I needed his steadiness, his warmth, his solid presence. It was late afternoon, and he would be at the tavern, probably finishing his shift. The thought of seeing him made my throat tight with a confusing mix of relief and guilt. I'd missed him so much – but I'd also nearly kissed someone else. The memory of that moment with Traola made shame burn hot in my chest. Even though nothing had happened, even though Traola had stopped it, the fact that I'd wanted it felt like a betrayal.

I pushed the feeling aside. I couldn't deal with that now. Right now, I just needed to feel safe.

I tied Copper up outside the tavern, my hands shaking as I worked the knots. He'd been so patient with me these past few days, so gentle, as if he understood I was hurt. I made sure he had a bucket of water to drink from, and as I straightened up, adjusting it so he could reach more easily, I looked up...

And there was Nikola – stood in the doorway of the tavern, wiping his hands on his apron, probably coming out to greet whoever had just arrived. When he saw me, his whole face transformed – surprise, joy, relief flooding across his features. His mouth opened to call my name, but before he could speak, before he could take more than a step towards me, I broke.

All the tears I'd been holding back for days came pouring out in wrenching sobs. My legs nearly gave out, and suddenly Nikola was there, catching me, pulling me against his chest as I fell completely apart.

"Elenah," he said, his arms wrapped tightly around me. "Elenah, I've got you. You're home. You're safe."

"I missed you," I choked out between sobs, clutching at his shirt like a drowning person clutching a rope. "I missed you so much. Nikola, I..."

"Shh... I know. I know." His hand stroked my hair, gentle and soothing, and his familiar scent surrounded me. "I missed you too. Every day. I'm so glad you're back."

I loved him. Gods, I loved him so much it hurt. This was home – these arms, this voice, this steady, reliable presence that had been the foundation of my life for three years. The guilt about Traola surged again, sharp and painful, but I pushed it down. Later. I'd deal with it later. Right now I just needed this, needed him, needed to feel like I hadn't lost everything.

"Father," I managed to gasp out. "Is he..."

"Still alive," Nikola said quickly, understanding immediately what I was asking. "He's still ill, still weak, but he's fighting. Your mother... she's been amazing, Elenah. So strong. I've been taking soup to them, checking on them every day."

Relief and fear warred in my chest. Alive. He was still alive. There was still time. There had to be time.

"Come inside," Nikola said gently, loosening

his hold on me just enough to look down at my face. His expression shifted from relief to concern as he took in my appearance – the bruises I hadn't managed to hide, the healing cut on my lip, the hollow look in my eyes. "You need food and rest. And you need to tell me what happened to you."

He took my hand – that simple, familiar gesture making fresh tears spring to my eyes – and led me into the tavern. The interior was warm and dim, only a few patrons scattered at the tables since it was that lull between afternoon and evening. The fire crackled in the hearth, and the smell of bread and soup made my stomach clench with sudden hunger.

Nikola guided me to a table near the fire and called out to the kitchen. "Marta! Can you bring food and water? And come sit with us when you can?"

Within moments, Marta appeared. The middle-aged elven woman took one look at me, and her face creased with concern.

"Sweet girl, you look half-dead," she said, but there was warmth in her voice. "Let me get you sorted."

She disappeared back into the kitchen and returned with a large mug of water, fresh bread, cheese, and a steaming bowl of soup. The scent was irresistible.

"Thank you," I whispered.

Marta settled into a chair across from me whilst Nikola sat beside me, his hand finding mine under the table. "Now," Marta said kindly but firmly, "eat first. Then talk."

I obeyed, spooning the soup into my mouth with shaking hands. It was good – hearty and rich – but I could barely taste it. Still, I forced myself to eat, knowing I needed the strength. Nikola and Marta watched me with concern, not pushing, just letting me take my time.

When I'd eaten enough to ease the worst of the hunger, I set down my spoon and took a shaky breath. "I found help," I said, my voice rough. "I found people who taught me how to heal Father. But..."

And then it all came pouring out – the Sun Society, their revolutionary approach to healing, the collaborative techniques they'd taught me. I told them about sensing magical energy, about healing flowers and birds, about practising on simulated lung fever. I watched their eyes widen with amazement, saw their expressions shift from scepticism to wonder as I described everything I'd learnt.

"You mean we've all been lied to?" Marta asked, her voice tight with outrage. "All of us could learn this?"

"All of us," I confirmed. "The whole system – the Healers' Guild, the official training, the idea that only special people can use magic – it's all designed to keep power concentrated in a few hands."

Then, my voice breaking, I told them about the Guild enforcers. About how they'd surrounded me, pulled me from Copper's back, thrown me to the ground. About how they'd stolen everything. I showed them the bruises, the healing cut on my lip. Nikola's hand tightened painfully around mine, and Marta's face went white with fury.

"They did this to you?" Nikola's voice was low and dangerous, more angry than I'd ever heard him. "They hurt you?"

I nodded, fresh tears spilling down my cheeks. "They said Father's life didn't matter compared to maintaining their order."

"Evil," Marta uttered forcefully. "Absolute evil."

"I need to perform the collaborative healing technique on Father," I said, leaning forward urgently. "I need other people to work with me." I looked between them desperately. "I know it sounds impossible. I know you've been taught your whole lives that only healers can safely use magic. But I'm telling you it's not true. I've done it. I've felt the energy, I've healed living things. And I can teach you. But I need you to trust me."

Nikola and Marta exchanged a long look, some wordless communication passing between them. Then Marta turned back to me, her jaw set with determination.

"I'm in," she said firmly. "There's no way I'm going to sit back and watch an innocent man lose his life due to such awful bureaucracy. Not when I can do something about it."

"Me too," Nikola said immediately. "Of course

I'll help. Elenah, you don't even need to ask. Your father is a good man, and you... you've been through so much. If there's any chance we can save him, we're taking it."

The relief that washed over me was so intense it made me dizzy. "You believe me?"

"I believe you," Nikola said, bringing my hand to his lips and kissing it gently. "And I'm so proud of you. Going all that way, learning all of that, standing up to those Guild enforcers even after what they did to you... you're the bravest person I know."

The guilt surged again – I didn't deserve his faith, not after what had almost happened with Traola – but I pushed it down. Later. I would tell him everything later, when I had the strength to face what it meant. For now, I just let myself lean into him, drawing comfort from his solid presence.

"Tomorrow morning," Nikola said, his voice taking on that practical, organising tone he used when solving problems. "Marta and I will come to your parents' cottage. The four of us – you, your mother, Marta, and me – will work together to heal your father. You can show us what to do."

"You're sure?" I asked, looking at Marta. "The Guild said they have ways of dealing with people who practise these techniques. If they find out…"

"Let them try," Marta said fiercely. "I'm not afraid of some pompous officials who think they own magic."

I felt hope kindle in my chest for the first time since the attack. It wasn't over. The enforcers hadn't won. I had allies, people willing to stand with me, willing to break the rules to save a life.

"Thank you," I whispered, looking between them. "Thank you so much."

"That's what community is for," Marta said, reaching across the table to squeeze my other hand. "Taking care of each other when those in power won't. Your Sun Society friends have the right idea."

Nikola stood, pulling me gently to my feet. "Come on. Let me walk you and Copper home. Your parents need to see you, and you need rest. Tomorrow's going to be a big day."

# Chapter Thirteen

When I first saw Father again, the sight of him nearly broke me.

Nikola had walked me home, his steady presence the only thing keeping me upright. When we'd reached the cottage door, he'd squeezed my hand one last time and told me he'd see me in the morning. Then I'd stepped inside, and there was Mother – older somehow, worn down by weeks of worry and exhaustion – and beyond her, in the bedroom, Father.

He was alive. That was the first thing, the most important thing. But his condition had worsened dramatically. The greyish-green pallor had deepened, spreading from his face down his neck. His breathing was a terrible rattling wheeze. He'd lost weight, his frame gaunt beneath the blankets, and when he'd opened his eyes to look at me, the exhaustion in them had been profound.

"You came back," he'd whispered weakly.

"Of course," I'd said, kneeling beside his bed and taking his hand – so thin now, the bones sharp beneath papery skin. "And I learnt so much. Tomorrow, Father, we're going to make you well."

He'd smiled wearily, too tired to even ask what I meant, and drifted back into a fitful sleep.

Mother and I had stayed up late into the night whilst I explained everything – the Sun Society, the collaborative healing techniques, what I'd learnt about magic and energy. I'd told her about the attack, about losing all the blends and supplies, watching her face pale with horror and then harden with determination.

"So we can really do this?" she had asked, her voice trembling between hope and fear. "We can actually save him?"

"We can try," I'd said. "And I think... I think we have a real chance."

At the time, lying awake in my own bed after being away for so long, I'd thought the next day couldn't come soon enough. Every minute Father struggled was agony. But now that morning had arrived, now that I could hear voices outside and knew Nikola and Marta had come as promised, I felt terror mixing with my hope.

What if I'd forgotten something crucial? What if I couldn't teach them quickly enough? What if the attack had damaged something inside me, broken my connection to the magic I'd so recently discovered? What if we failed, and Father died knowing we'd tried and couldn't save him?

"They're here," Mother said from the doorway, and I could hear the barely contained emotion in her voice.

I found Nikola and Marta standing in our small front room, both looking determined and slightly nervous. Marta carried a basket of what looked like breakfast – bread and cheese and fruit – and Nikola's eyes found mine immediately, full of love and concern and unwavering support.

"Thank you," I said, my voice thick. "Thank

you both for coming. For believing me. For being willing to do this."

"Where else would we be?" Marta said firmly. "Now, let's get to work. That man in there needs us."

Mother clasped Marta's hand, tears streaming down her face. "I can't tell you what this means. You're risking so much..."

"We're not risking anything," Nikola interrupted gently. "We're doing what's right. That's all."

I gathered them around the small kitchen table, my hands shaking slightly as I tried to organise my thoughts. This was it. Everything had been leading to this – all the searching, all the learning, all the pain and loss and discovery – it all came down to this moment.

"I need to teach you the basics," I said. "It's going to be a crash course in something you've been told your whole lives is impossible. But I need you to trust me, and I need you to trust yourselves."

They nodded, their faces serious and attentive.

"Magic isn't dangerous, or mysterious, or limited to special people," I began, echoing Traola's words. "It's as natural as breathing. You've all been using it your whole lives without realising – every intuition, every gut feeling, every moment when you just knew something was true."

I watched their expressions shift from scepticism to wonder as I explained about magical energy, about the life force that flowed through all living things. I had them close their eyes and try to sense it, guiding them through the exercises the Sun Society had taught me.

"I feel something," Nikola said after a few minutes, his voice filled with awe. "It's like... like everything is humming."

"That's it exactly," I said, relief flooding through me. "That's the energy we're going to work with."

Mother gasped softly. "I can feel it too. Oh gods, I can actually feel it."

Marta nodded slowly. "It's there. I never noticed it before, but now that I'm paying attention... it's everywhere."

We spent the next hour practising – sensing the energy in plants, in each other, learning to distinguish between healthy and disrupted flow. I showed them how to direct their own energy, how to share it, how to work together. They were quick learners, driven by necessity and love, and I felt my confidence growing with each small success.

"Now," I said, my voice steady despite the enormity of the moment. "We're going to heal Father. Together."

We moved into the bedroom where Father lay sleeping. His breathing was worse than ever, each inhalation a struggle. I could feel the wrongness in his energy even from across the room – hot and chaotic and dangerously weak.

"Positions," I said.

They arranged themselves around the bed. Mother stood at Father's head, her hand resting gently on his brow. Nikola took position on Father's right side, Marta on his left. And I stood at the foot of the bed, ready to co-ordinate everything.

"Remember," I said, my voice low and calm

despite the terror thrumming through me. "We're not forcing anything. We're working with his body's natural healing processes. We're helping them along, encouraging them, supporting them."

"What do I focus on?" Mother asked, her voice shaking.

"You're managing pain and fever," I told her. "Let your energy feel cool and soothing. Nikola, you're reducing the inflammation in his lungs – think warm and encouraging, helping the swelling go down. Marta, you're clearing the congestion, helping him breathe – your energy should flow like water, washing away what doesn't belong."

"And you?" Nikola asked.

"I'm holding it all together," I said. "Co-ordinating, harmonising. Making sure we work as one instead of four separate people." I took a deep breath. "Are we ready?"

They nodded, and I could see the determination in their faces, the love. This was what the Sun Society had meant about community – people coming together, supporting each other, refusing to accept that suffering was inevitable.

I closed my eyes and reached out with my magical senses, feeling for Father's energy. The disruption was worse up close – his life force flickering like a candle in a storm, the inflammation in his lungs burning hot and angry, the fever throwing everything off balance. For a moment, the enormity of what we were attempting threatened to overwhelm me.

But then I felt the others reaching out too. Mother's energy – cool and gentle, like a soothing cloth on fevered skin. Nikola's warmth – steady and encouraging, so perfectly him. Marta's flowing presence – practical and efficient.

"That's it," I murmured. "Now, let me weave us together."

I reached out with my own energy and began to co-ordinate, connecting their efforts into one harmonious whole. It was like conducting music, finding the way each voice could complement the others. Mother's cooling presence balanced Nikola's warmth.

Marta's flowing energy carried away what they loosened. And I held the centre, keeping everything moving in the right direction.

For several minutes, nothing seemed to happen. Father's breathing remained laboured, his colour unchanged. Doubt crept in – what if I was doing it wrong? What if I'd missed something important?

Then I felt it – a subtle shift in Father's energy. The inflammation beginning to ease, just slightly. The fever starting to break. The congestion loosening.

"It's working," I whispered. "Keep going. Just like that."

But the effort was immense. I could feel my own energy draining, the co-ordination taking more out of me than I'd expected. My knees began to shake, and heat rose in my head. The room swam slightly, and fear clawed at my throat. What if I wasn't strong enough? What if I collapsed before we finished?

Then Nikola's hand found mine, squeezing gently without breaking his focus. I felt his love and support flowing through that touch, shoring me up, reminding me I wasn't alone. Mother's determination washed over me, fierce and unwavering – she would not lose her husband, not after coming this far. And Marta's steady presence grounded me, practical and sure.

They were all here, all fighting with me. I wasn't carrying this alone.

I pushed through the weakness, through the fear, and poured everything I had into co-ordinating our efforts. Minutes stretched into what felt like hours. My whole world narrowed to the flow of energy, to Father's struggling life force, to the slow, gradual improvement we were creating together.

And then...

Father took a breath that didn't rattle.

My eyes flew open. His colour was changing, the greyish-green tinge fading, replaced by something closer to his natural tone. His breathing was still laboured, but it was easier, deeper. The terrible tension in his features was relaxing.

"Don't stop," I said urgently. "We're not done yet."

We kept working, and with each passing minute, the improvements became more visible. The fever broke in a wave of sweat that soaked through his nightshirt. The inflammation in his lungs continued to recede, and his breathing grew progressively easier. The congestion that had rattled in his chest began to clear, expelled in a few productive coughs that made Mother cry out with relief.

Finally, after what might have been thirty minutes or three hours – I'd lost all sense of time – I felt Father's energy stabilise. Not perfect, not completely healed, but stable. Strong enough. Out of immediate danger.

"We can stop," I said, my voice cracking.

We all stepped back, and for a moment no one could speak. Father's breathing was clear and steady. His colour was nearly normal. As we watched, his eyes fluttered open – truly open, clear and aware for the first time in weeks.

"Miriel?" he said, his voice weak but recognisable. "What... what happened?"

"You're going to be all right." Mother collapsed to her knees beside the bed, sobbing as she clutched his hand. "Oh, Jorik, you're going to be all right."

Father's eyes found mine, and they were full of questions and wonder. "Elenah? Did you...?"

"We all did," I said, tears streaming down my face. "All of us together. We saved you, Father."

I looked around – at Mother weeping with relief, at Marta wiping her eyes with the back of her hand, at Nikola with his arm around my shoulders, his face wet with tears and bright with joy. We were all exhausted, emotionally wrung out, barely able to stand. But we were elated. We were victorious.

We had done what Healer Morvaine had refused to do. What the Guild enforcers had tried to stop. What the entire system was designed to prevent.

We had saved a life through love and co-operation and the refusal to accept that some people were meant to die whilst others held all the power.

"I can't believe it worked," Marta said, laughing through her tears. "We actually healed him."

"You're amazing," Nikola said to me, pulling me close. "You're all amazing. This is... this is everything."

Father coughed again, but it was a healthy cough, clearing his lungs. He looked around at all of us with something like awe. "What you've done... what you've learnt..."

"Is available to everyone," I said firmly. "That's what I learnt, Father. Magic isn't special or rare. It's not limited to healers with official training. It belongs to all of us. This – what we just did – anyone could learn it."

"Then you have to teach them," Father said, his voice growing stronger with each word. "You have to show people what's possible. Elenah, you have to..."

"Hush," Mother said, still crying, still holding his hand. "Rest now. We'll work out the next step later. For now, just rest and heal."

But as I looked around at everyone – at these people who had believed me, who had trusted me, who had broken every rule they'd been taught – I knew Father was right. This couldn't stop here. What we'd done today proved that the system was built on lies and that ordinary people could do extraordinary things if they were given the chance.

We had saved one life today. But maybe, just maybe, we could save more.

# Chapter Fourteen

Still riding high on the emotion of having healed Father – the impossible made real, the miracle we'd created together – I knew I couldn't put it off any longer. The guilt had been gnawing at me, and now that Father was safe and the immediate crisis had passed, I had to face what I'd been avoiding.

I had to tell Nikola about Traola.

The four of us had stayed in Father's room for a while longer, marvelling at his recovery. He'd drifted back to sleep, but it was real sleep now – restful and healing – not the fitful, fevered haze he'd been trapped in for weeks.

"We'll give you some time alone," I said softly to Mother.

Mother's eyes were still red from crying, but her smile was radiant. "Thank you, darling. Thank you for everything. For not giving up. For being so brave."

"I should get back to the tavern," Marta said diplomatically, gathering her things. "The lunchtime customers will be there soon." She gave me a warm hug, whispering in my ear, "You did good, girl. Real good."

After Marta left, I turned to Nikola. "Will you walk with me?"

Something in my tone must have alerted him, because his expression grew more serious. But he just nodded and took my hand. "Of course."

We walked in silence through Miltoven's familiar streets, past the houses I'd known my whole life, towards the old oak tree with its wooden swing bench. Our spot. The place where we'd spent countless evenings, talking about everything and nothing, dreaming about the future, learning the comfortable rhythms of being together.

The chains creaked as we settled onto the

worn seat, and Nikola set it in gentle motion with his foot – the same gesture he'd made a thousand times before. But my heart was racing, my palms sweating despite the relatively cool air.

I looked at him – really looked at him – and felt tears prick at my eyes. He was so beautiful, with his strong features and kind eyes, the sunlight catching in his dark hair. And more than beautiful, he was good. Patient and steady and loyal. He'd waited for me, worried about me, taken care of my parents in my absence. He'd believed me when I told him impossible things, had risked himself to help heal Father.

And I was about to hurt him.

"Nikola," I began, my voice already shaking. "I need to tell you something that happened whilst I was away. Something I should have told you already."

He turned to face me fully, his expression open and attentive. "Ok."

"There was someone at the Sun Society," I said, forcing the words out. "A woman named

Traola. She was the one who taught me most of what I learnt. She was… she was incredible. Passionate and smart and committed to helping people. And I…" The tears spilt over, running hot down my cheeks. "I developed feelings for her. Romantic feelings."

Nikola's expression didn't change. He just listened, patient as always.

"Nothing happened," I continued quickly, desperately. "I mean, almost – on my last night there, I tried to kiss her. But she stopped it. She said she wouldn't come between us, between you and me." I was crying harder now, the words tumbling out in a rush. "But I wanted to. I wanted to kiss her. And I'm so sorry, Nikola. I'm so, so sorry. You were here waiting for me, and I was developing feelings for someone else, and I feel so guilty and confused and…"

"Elenah," Nikola said softly, interrupting my spiral. "Look at me."

I raised my eyes to his, expecting to see hurt or anger or betrayal. But his face was calm, his eyes warm with understanding.

"You're not upset?" I asked, bewildered.

A small smile tugged at his lips. "Should I be?"

"I just told you I had romantic feelings for someone else!" Fresh tears spilt down my cheeks. "I almost kissed her! How can you not be hurt?"

Nikola reached up and gently wiped away my tears with his thumbs, his hands cradling my face. "Because I know you, Elenah. And I've always known that you have a deeply loving soul. The propensity to love... it's one of the most beautiful things about you."

"But..."

"Listen to me," he said, firm but kind. "You went through something extraordinary. You met people who changed your worldview, who taught you things you never imagined possible, who believed in you when you needed it most. Of course you developed strong feelings for them. Of course you felt connected to Traola especially – she guided you, supported you, showed you what you were capable of."

"That doesn't make it ok," I protested weakly.

"It makes it natural," Nikola said. "Elenah, love isn't a finite resource. Your capacity to care deeply about people, to admire them, to feel drawn to them – that doesn't diminish what we have. It never could."

I stared at him, unable to fully process what he was saying. "You're really not angry?"

"I'm not angry," he confirmed. "I know your love for me is strong and eternal. I've never doubted that, not for a second. The fact that you're capable of loving others – of appreciating them, feeling connected to them – that beautiful openness of heart could never make me doubt your love for me."

"How can you be so understanding?" I asked, my voice breaking. "How can you be so... so good?"

"Because I love you," Nikola said simply. "And part of loving you is accepting all of you – including your generous heart and your capacity to care deeply about people. You didn't betray me, Elenah. You experienced something profound, and you felt complicated things as a result. And then you came home and told me the truth, even though you were scared. That's not betrayal. That's honesty."

The relief that washed over me was so intense it left me breathless. I'd been carrying this weight, this guilt, certain it would damage or destroy what we had. But Nikola was right – he knew me. He understood me in a way that went deeper than jealousy or possession.

"It's you I want," I said fiercely, grabbing his hands. "No matter what I felt for Traola, or how confused I was – I want you. You're home. You're safety. You're everything steady and real in my life. I love you, Nikola. I love you so much."

"I know," he said, smiling now. "And I love you. That hasn't changed. It will never change."

"I feel the same," I said. "I promise you, I feel the same."

He pulled me close, wrapping his arms around me, and I buried my face in his shoulder. We sat like that for a long moment, the swing creaking gently beneath us, the sun warm on our backs. I felt the tension I'd been carrying finally melt away.

"Thank you," I murmured against his chest. "For understanding. For being so... so impossibly patient and kind."

"That's what love does," he said. "It makes room for complexity, for growth, for the messy, complicated reality of what it means to be alive."

We adjusted our positions so we could sit side by side, his arm around my shoulders, my head resting against him. Nikola began to sing then, his voice low and soft – a gentle melody I'd heard him hum before, but never with words. It was a song about coming home, about finding peace after a long journey, about love that endures through change and challenge.

As his beautiful voice wrapped around me, I thought about how grateful I was for how everything had turned out. I was grateful for Nikola, Mother, Father, and Marta. Grateful to have found the Sun Society and learnt so much from them. Grateful to be alive, whole, and capable of making a difference.

And with that gratitude came responsibility. The responsibility to use what I'd learnt, to share what I knew, to challenge the systems that caused unnecessary suffering. It wouldn't be easy, but as Nikola's song faded and we sat together in our familiar spot, I felt something settle in my bones. Purpose. Direction. Hope.

# Epilogue

Within weeks, word spread throughout Miltoven like wildfire. The story was too remarkable to contain: I had saved Father, and more astonishingly, I'd done it with the help of ordinary people who'd discovered they possessed magic all along. Every retelling added another layer of vindication for those who'd suffered under the old system, and another crack in the foundation of the Guild's authority.

Healer Morvaine disappeared from the village one misty morning, leaving no forwarding address and taking only what she could carry. Some said it was shame that drove her away – the humiliation of having her petty cruelty exposed and her authority so thoroughly undermined. Others suspected she feared the anger of villagers who were beginning to calculate how many loved ones they'd lost to her monopolistic control. Either way, she was never seen in Miltoven again, and few mourned her departure.

The Guild, perhaps recognising the danger of creating martyrs, didn't dare intervene directly. By the time they might have considered action, Nikola, Marta and I, along with a growing circle of enthusiastic villagers, were already teaching healing techniques to anyone who wanted to learn. The evidence was overwhelming and undeniable – in cosy living rooms throughout Miltoven, ordinary elves were channelling healing energy, mending injuries, and caring for one another without any official sanction or permission.

When Nikola and I made the journey to thank the Sun Society, we found the settlement buzzing with excitement. News of Miltoven's transformation had already reached them, and they welcomed us as heroes of our own story. I'd been nervous about Nikola meeting Traola, worried there might be awkwardness or tension – but I needn't have been. Watching them talk and laugh together, seeing how naturally they got along, filled me with a quiet joy I hadn't expected. There were no awkward feelings at all, just mutual love and understanding – for me and for the greater good of everything we were trying to achieve. Traola told Nikola stories about my training that made him laugh, and he sang for the settlement that evening, his beautiful voice bringing tears to many eyes. It was perfect, and it healed something in me I hadn't realised still needed healing.

"You did more than save your father," Traola told me with obvious pride during that visit. "You proved that our methods work in the real world, with real people, under real pressure. That's more valuable than a thousand theoretical discussions."

The ripple effects spread far beyond Miltoven. Other villages heard the story and began questioning why they too were dependent on single healers who might refuse treatment on a whim. Small groups began seeking out the Sun Society, not as rebels or outcasts, but as teachers of essential knowledge that had been deliberately withheld.

The Guild tried to maintain control through

increasingly desperate measures – new regulations, threats of consequences, attempts to discredit the collaborative healing methods. But their credibility had been shattered. Once people understood that the Guild's power rested entirely on manufactured ignorance, their authority continued to diminish.

Within a couple of years, the Healers' Guild had effectively disbanded. Some of its members, recognising the changing tide, publicly apologised and offered to share their knowledge freely. Others retreated into bitter isolation, clinging to their defunct titles and refusing to accept that their era had ended. But most simply adapted, finding new roles in a world where healing belonged to everyone.

The Sun Society, once dismissed as dangerous anarchists and seditionists, became something of legend. Their story was told in every corner of elven civilisation – how a small group of idealists in the forest had kept alive the truth that magic belonged to all, not just a privileged few.

Father lived for many more happy years, his

illness nothing but a distant memory. I watched him grow old with Mother by his side. But perhaps more importantly, an entire generation of children grew up believing they had the power to take care of themselves and their neighbours. The rigid hierarchies that had once seemed natural and necessary gradually gave way to networks of mutual support and shared responsibility.

Nikola and I married one golden autumn day, surrounded by everyone we loved – my parents, Marta, and several members of the Sun Society who travelled to be with us. Traola was there, and she and Nikola laughed together like old friends. It was everything a wedding should be: joyful, meaningful, and full of hope for the future.

As the years went by, in taverns and marketplaces throughout the land, people told stories about a young elven woman who defied convention to save her father's life – and ended up saving much more than that. Sometimes I heard these stories myself, often embellished beyond recognition, and I would smile quietly, remembering the terrified girl who'd left Miltoven all those years ago.

The stories grew and spread, carrying with them the revolutionary idea that ordinary people possessed extraordinary capabilities – they just needed someone to remind them of what was always there, always inside.

The sun, it seemed, was rising everywhere. And once people had seen its light, they couldn't be convinced to live in darkness again.

www.ingramcontent.com/pod-product-compliance
Lightning Source LLC
Chambersburg PA
CBHW032003180726
48283CB00008B/2547